Ruth Snyder

Wtch
10.⁰⁰

A Day in Regensburg

translated from the Yiddish
by Jacob Sloan

A Day in
Regensburg

short stories by

JOSEPH OPATOSHU

The Jewish Publication Society of America
Philadelphia • *5728/1968*

Copyright © 1968
By the Jewish Publication Society of America
All Rights Reserved   First Edition
Library of Congress Catalog Card Number: 68-15788
Manufactured in the United States of America
Designed by Adrianne Onderdonk Dudden

Contents

Continuity:
A Memory of my Father

Four rooms, atop a four flight walk up, look out upon Crotona Park that sprawls below in Bronx, New York. Against a wall, framed by two windows, stands the oak-wood writing desk. Through the open windows a steady flow of golden sun, rounded hillocks, green-tipped trees and bluish splash from tiny, shimmering Indian Lake.

At the desk, his massive shoulders bent across the blue-lined writing pad, sits the youthful father. Forehead, nose and chin a sweep of blade-honed sharpness. His sledgelike hand clutches the bellied fountain pen as he hammers, hews and chisels words and phrases, faces, pictures, people upon the cold, white paper pad.

His eyes, deep pools of warm, brown velvet, look up, stare into the vastness that surrounds him. Little park Crotona becomes an endless stretch of ageless Polish forests, while placid, rounded Indian Lake flows mightily as does the Polish Vistula.

Beneath the desk, between the legs of the father's chair, sits the little boy amidst a mass of pots and pans, a long wooden mixing spoon clutched in chubby hands. He, too, hews and hammers, beats a wild staccato drum, weaves and spins anew the thrice-told tales of father's stories about forest robbers, hairy bears and white-fanged wolves, giant Jews with wooly beards riding wild and proud on fiery prancing steeds.

The father pens a period to final word of line just written. He drops the pen, rises from the chair and bends to boy beneath the desk. He grabs the blond-haired little one and, enveloping him in his arms, throws himself into a stomping, lumbering, bearish dance that carries both from room to room of the sun-drenched, fourth-floor home. Peals of bubbling laughter from the little one, booming, rolling laughter from the father as he dances, shouting: "Hop! Hop! Hop!" And across the written pages on the table-top, sun rays hop and dance between the sentences, among the words and densely written letters that are Yiddish.

The laughing boy grabs the father's pointed chin and, shaking lustily, yells: "Papa, tell me another story, a terrible, scary story!"

The father seats himself upon a studio couch, enfolds the boy in warm, protective arms and tells of grandpas and of grandmas, tells of forests and of towns, of Uncle Yukeff's fights with Cossacks, horses, bears and wolves and imps. Boy in arms gulps and swallows thirstily the stories, and within the curly head, grandpas, grandmas and impish bears, spin and weave along with towns and forests, horses, uncles and Cossacks. Eyes grow ever bigger, wider, full red lips are slightly parted, as they drink and swallow song of father, melody of generations, ageless chant of continuity.

Suddenly the father stops, puts four fingers to his lips and blows a blast, a Shofar peal! A roar of joyous laughter from the two, as once again the father lifts his son up high and, dancing wildly, gallops round the room.

Laughter from the little boy. Laughter from the young-yeared father. Laughter from the rays of sun as they dance among the black-penned letters, dance between the words of Yiddish, as they sing their song of life.

The fountain pen flies across the blue-lined pad, leaving a trail of flowing, racing words and sentences. The impatient, anguished letters twist and leap ahead of the moving pen-point as though the hand could not keep up with the outpouring of black-ink images that stream from the figure bent across the writing desk:

". . . and when his wife and daughter handed him a package containing a change of shirt and socks and underwear, Reb Shloime, ritual slaughterer of the town of Mlawa, looked dry-eyed round the room.

"Before him stood young Motke, his former assistant, now almost unrecognizable in Polish uniform, steel helmet pushed back off his forehead. Next to him, his eighteen-year-old daughter Ruchel, black braids framing the shimmering blackness of

*her eyes. Alongside Ruchel stood his Chana, twenty
years of life between them.*

"*The four gazed at each other with burning,
searing eyes. This was the moment.*

"*Motke, retreating with the Polish infantry, had
stopped to take Reb Shloime with him. He knew
that the advancing German Panzers would reach
Mlawa in a matter of minutes. And when the
Germans hit a town, the first thing done was to
murder every able-bodied Jewish male. He came
to save Reb Shloime.*

"*A second passed, another, as the eyes clung and
clutched and clamored until a helpless moan escaped from Chana, to be echoed by a stifled groan
from Ruchel.*

"*Choking back the lump that stood in throat
and eyes, Reb Shloime whispered to his wife:*

"'*Chanale, where is my Shofar?*'

"'*What do you want with a ram's horn at this
time?*' *Motke questioned hoarsely.* '*Forgive me, Reb
Shloime, but the hangmen are breathing down our
necks. Ruchel, tell him we have to get moving.*'

"*A thin smile flew fleetingly across Reb
Shloime's lips.* '*You're right, Motke, you're right. But
today is Rosh Hashana and a Jew must blow the
Shofar on Rosh Hashana. Chanale, my Shofar.*'

"*Chana couldn't move. Ruchel turned quickly,
crossed to a bureau, opened a top drawer and from
its depths brought out a ram's horn wrapped in
silken cloth. She handed it to her father.*

"*The ritual slaughterer crossed to a window and
threw open the shutters. The first faint rays of dawn*

trickled across the window sill. In the near distance the thunderous roar of the advancing tanks hung over the countryside.

"Reb Shloime placed himself within the window and, Shofar at his lips, faced the mechanized might.

"A Shofar blast ripped the air, a second, a third and when he reached the last and final piercing peal that sought to scream its way beyond the seventh heaven of the Almighty, tears streamed from Chana's eyes, from Ruchel's eyes, from Motke's eyes and tears fell upon the hand that clutched the Shofar at Reb Shloime's lips. . . ."

A deep and shattering cry races through the body of the man as he drops his fountain pen and falls across the thickly written pages on his oak-wood desk. The curved, still massive back heaves and trembles as he chokes within him tears and moans that wrack his body, while on the wall, above the desk, from out a black-wood frame, an eternal, flying Chagall-Jew clutches a Torah and weeps along with the knotted figure at the desk below.

The book-lined room looks out upon the placid majesty of Hudson River as it flows beside the green treed bank of Riverside Drive in the summer of 1942.

A tall thin figure, in uniform of olive-drab, crosses the room and stands quietly beside the bent and crumpled man.

"Pop, what is it?"

The deep set eyes jerk upward with embarrassment. A hand reaches quickly for a handkerchief in trouser pocket and vigorously wipes and

xii

rubs the salty dampness from ample nose and
swollen eyes. Smiling sheepishly, he thrusts the handkerchief into his pocket and says:

"It's nothing, nothing. Foolishness. Your father
indulged himself a little."

A shadow crosses his face, anxiety fills the eyes
as the reality of soldier-son's presence in the room hits
him forcefully.

"It's time?"

"Time."

Pounding silence between son and father. Eyes
bore into eyes as each one searches for screaming, unsaid, ageless answer. As each one cries the universal
cry. The father: "I should go, I. I brought him
into this world and raised him for this madness."
While son thinks: "I will go and I'll return for I've
a life to live ahead of me."

They fall into each other's arms, clinging almost
unto desperation and still the unsaid stays unspoken,
yet answer rises from between them. The answer lies
in town Mlawa, lies in Shofar of Reb Shloime, in
inky stream upon the paper, in flying Jew who
clutches a Torah.

The father kisses his son gently on the lips and
whispers hoarsely, "We must go. Your wife and
mother will be waiting."

He slips into a summer jacket and both together
head for the door. Suddenly the father stops, slaps
himself upon the forehead and smiles up to his son,
"See, your Pop is getting old, forgot my keys and
fountain pen."

He runs back to his writing desk as son gazes

slowly round the rooms, drinking in the all-familiar books and pictures, radio and candlesticks, bag and baggage of a lifetime.

At the rise of a rolling acre stands a four room, white- and green-trimmed bungalow. Within the living room, between French windows, a bamboo table shaded by a leafy oak beyond. August heat hangs heavily within the room. It is summer 1950 at Croton-Falls, New York.

Pen in hand, he muses. The massive rounded back, a little rounder. The high-swept forehead, now a little higher as grayness curls among the blackness of receding hair.

The deep, warm eyes look out beyond the windows, oaks and rolling countryside. The eyes sweep on beyond the borders of the land, span seas and oceans, desert drifts and mountain cliffs, and come to rest atop the fortress in Judea. Betar, last bastion of Bar Kochba, the final stand of Jewish revolutionaries against the might of Rome. He sees the sage Akiba as he wrestles with decisions, searches for an answer to the question that is final. "To fight till all go down in blaze of glory to become a burning legend of resistance. Or else surrender, and, surrendering, protect the word, maintain the thought, give life to everlasting drive of man for freedom."

A gleeful shout of childish laughter rolls down the acre to the house, cuts through the heat and revery.

"Oppy! Oppy! I'm riding down to you on horsey Lima-Googoo. Oppy, come and see!"

Hastily he drops the pen upon the table and trots through the kitchen to the screened rear door.

Atop the shoulders of his laughing, panting son rides the little one. Hanging on to father's head, the three-year-old bounces merrily and shouts to Oppy:

"See, I told you my horse Lima-Googoo came to see me. I think he needs a drink of water. He sounds thirsty."

Suddenly the father bends his head and off his shoulders brown-haired squealing boy comes flying, into the open arms of grandpa.

"Hop, hop! Hop, hop!" The grandpa shouts as, cradling the boy within his arms, he throws himself into a stomping, lumbering, bearish dance that carries both across the lawn beneath the coolness of the willow trees.

Laughter from the little boy, laughter from the grandpa Oppy, laughter of a memory within the eyes of son, now father.

Little boy with dancing eyes grabs the grandpa's pointed chin and lustily demands a story.

Beneath the shade of willow tree lie grandpa, grandson on the grass, and storyteller spins his story of towns and forests, imps and horses, grandpas, grandmas and of fighting Uncle Yukeffs.

Eyes of boy grow ever wider as he swims along with song of grandpa. And his father sits beside them, listening to melody of generations, ageless chant of continuity.

David Opatoshu

A Day in Regensburg

A Day in Regensburg

The ponderous synagogue doors, bearing the forged and beaten emblem of the Shield of David, stood wide open. The cool shadows within extended to the plastered entranceway, where cooing doves rocked on their small red feet.

On the pulpit stood old Yekel, who had passed along the office of sexton to his son. The old man's feeble face was wrinkled and sunken with age. Tangled and matted, his white beard grew to his very eyebrows, creating the grotesque impression that his face was garlanded by a wreath of garlic.

Yekel regarded the red carpet spread between the pulpit and the Holy Ark, the embellished candelabra and glass lamps, the scrubbed, white pews, the freshened walls decorated with paintings of deer, musical instruments, and verses from the Book of Psalms. The old sexton was pleased: the Ark curtains and the mantles covering the Torah Scrolls within the Ark had been thoroughly aired, and not a speck of dust was visible anywhere in the synagogue. He sucked in his lips, sniffed as though on the verge of sneezing, and said to his son in a high voice:

"Praised be the Name of the Blessed Lord,

when will we have such a marriage feast here again? Such an event happens once in a lifetime. To think that our most eminent man, our own mettlesome Samuel Belasser, should be arranging a marriage with his peer, wealthy Elijah Margolis of Worms! It would do you no harm to listen to me, Berl!"

"I *am* listening, Father." His son moved his gnome-like, bell-shaped gray hat, and continued cutting the burned tips of the tallow candles.

"How runs the old saying, Berl? 'It's one thing to talk and another thing to act.'" The old man pulled up his knee trousers above the long woolen stockings. "Remember, these two communities, Regensburg and Worms, long the most prominent in all of Ashkenaz,* have not been on speaking terms the last few years. But now, Berl, we will have peace, for Regensburg is betrothing Worms. We will be having a merry time, I tell you; there'll be drumming and humming aplenty. They say the Prague jesters are coming to the wedding, and our own Leib of Regensburg has been readying for the event since Passover. He has songs to sing and stories to tell. The one thing which surprises me is that the beggars haven't turned up yet. They're not fond of synagogue-going, but those folk are always first to arrive at these affairs."

Berl, scrawny and stunted in growth, suddenly straightened up and grew lively, his sparse blond beard thrusting out with the sense of its power, like the tail feathers of a cock about to crow.

* Germany

"Is it true, Father, that Samuel Belasser has already squandered ten thousand reichsthaler on the wedding?"

"He could squander twenty thousand." His father thrust two fingers in the shape of a pincer at his son, missing Berl's jutting beard by a hair.

Eyes sparkling, a smile on both their lips, father and son stood thus with heads raised for a full moment.

Old Yekel gazed at the colored panes above the Holy Ark. The burning rays of the sun, filtering through the panes, merged with the happy twittering of sparrows to echo in the corners of the empty synagogue. As a boy, Yekel had believed that the chants of the prayer leader ascended to heaven through these floral panes set deep above the Holy Ark. And who could gainsay it?

With measured steps the old man left the synagogue.

In the vestibule, dark and cool as a cellar, stood a round, dented, copper wash basin. Around the taps and pipes, where Jews by the hundreds had dipped their fingers, the copper was worn away.

Out of habit, the old sexton wiped his hands on the damp copper, and his lips began to murmur. For Yekel, the laver was no broken vessel. Here, at the worn taps, had stood generations of families, households. All of Regensburg surrounding the synagogue courtyard came to his mind at that moment —buildings named "The Crown," "The White Deer," "The Sun"; buildings over which to this day hung signs depicting a Black Bear, a Green Door, a Red Door, a Spring Well; all of Jew Street, the mortuary of the chapel, the graveyard on the hill—all of these came to life for a moment in the consciousness of the sexton; they were all waiting for him outside, flooded in sunlight. Certainly, the seventy years of Yekel's life had not been in vain. The years lived on in the synagogue, at the laver in the vestibule, in the Golden Lion, where Yekel dwelt, in every object in his home, even in the sand under his feet.

The sexton went out into the courtyard. His weak ears could barely discern the singsong chanting that issued from the yeshiva next door to the synagogue. He sat himself down on a bench next to his six-year-old grandson, a barefoot lad who was basking in the sun.

"How came you here, Daniel?" The sexton loosened the high collar of the short, pleated coat that fell to his waist. "Should you not be in the schoolroom?"

"The Master has set us free for the day," replied the lad, sidling over to his grandfather. "No lessons today, there's a wedding in town."

"Indeed there is—you are right, my lad," said the old man, embracing the youngster.

The day turned blue and gold.

The sun stood overhead, its flames engulfing the clouds. The synagogue, with its arched roof and walls of rough-hewn stone crumbling with age, seemed veined with silver and gold. All things appeared to be reaching up toward the sky to enjoy the heat; every secret nook and cranny basked in the benevolent eye of the sun. The church spires of Saint Amram shone brilliantly above the synagogue cupola.

Embracing his grandson, the old Regensburg sexton pointed out the church, and went on to inform him that the city of Cologne had from days of antiquity been renowned for its yeshiva. Many, many hundreds of years ago, Rabbi Amram, one of the saints of Ashkenaz, and a great cabalist to boot, had been the head of the Cologne yeshiva. It was he, Rabbi Amram, who by invoking combinations and permutations of the Ineffable Name, had called up Messiah, the son of Joseph. The Messiah had been ready to destroy the entire universe. But, Rabbi Amram, in his compassion for all living things, man, and beast, and bird—why, his compassion was such that he never in all his life tasted food until his birds had first been fed. . . .

As Yekel spoke, his grandson stretched out on the bench. He sent his arms and legs sprawling, content with the warm sun, with the old man's hands cooling his cheeks, curling his earlocks, stroking his forehead.

The words falling from Yekel's sunken mouth rose in a singsong, and circled before the lad's eyes. He had heard this tale more than once. But now, as always, with the very first words, Daniel felt his body grow lighter and lighter, soaring from the bench to pursue the words, the melancholy cadence that fluttered overhead, to mingle with the twitter of the sparrows and the cooing of the doves.

The lad anticipated his grandfather, urging him on with his shrill voice:

"And when Rabbi Amram's last hour was about to expire . . ."

"Yes, dear child," and Yekel chose his words carefully, as though pronouncing them aloud from a manuscript. "When Rabbi Amram's last hour was about to expire, he sent for his disciples. And he said to them: 'My dear disciples, when I am dead, purify my body according to the ancient usage of our people, and lay me in a coffin, and lay the coffin in a small vessel, and set the small vessel on the river Rhine. Then let the vessel sail where it lists. It will bear me to the place where my father and mother lie buried.' And just as soon as the disciples laid the coffin in the vessel on the Rhine, the vessel moved, against the wind, sailing until it came to Mayence. There the whole city—Jew and Gentile —came running to see the wonder. Now, when the Gentiles tried to lay hold of the vessel, it evaded them. But when the Jews approached the shores of the Rhine, the vessel made straight for them. From which it was clear that it belonged to the Jews, and not to the Gentiles. Then the Gentiles were filled with a cruel rage, and they beat the Jews in their wrath—and the bishop ordered a chapel to be built over the coffin. That, my child, is the place of dese-cration known to this day as 'the impurity of Amram.' "

"And the head of the yeshiva?" inquired his grandson, opening wide a pair of clear blue eyes, as though ignorant of the story's end. "Does the head of the yeshiva still lie in that place of desecration?"

"No, Daniel. That night, his disciples took Rabbi Amram's body out of the coffin and brought it to our graveyard for a proper burial."

"And you, Grandfather, do you know where the grave is?" The lad slipped a bare foot into one of the slippers that had fallen off Yekel's feet.

"No one knows, dear child." For Yekel was the only one who knew that secret nowadays. Tomorrow he would take Berl with him to the cemetery and show him where Rabbi Amram lay buried. He, Yekel, had been told the secret, receiving it as an inheritance from his father; his father had heard it from his, and his from his, and thus it had been transmitted from generation to generation. He would make Berl take an oath to keep the burial place a lifelong secret. And when Berl grew old? Why, God be praised, there was the grandson, Daniel.

Torn and tattered, yeshiva boys shot out of the academy. They could not resist running after the long hours of confinement.

"I haven't had a bite to eat today!"

"I've been on a fast since yesterday!"

"I'm dead sleepy. All today and yesterday I've been copying the Master's latest scholarly commentary!"

"That makes you an author overnight!"

"Not I, Moshel. One author is enough—you preening yourself with the borrowed feathers of other people's ideas in your collection of notes."

"But first I have to eat!" Moshel held his belly.

"What a cavity!"

"And what a paunch!"

"There's none as big as Moshel's in all Regensburg!"

"He is fixing to gorge and swill!"

"Lemeline the caterer says," Moshel pretended innocence, "there are all kinds of good things to be served at Belasser's—roasted meat and broiled meat, stuffing and Italian macaroni, fish in sweet and sour sauces, and herring in wine."

"Then what are we hanging around here for?"

"Let's be off!"

"Here is Yekel, Yekel the sexton."

"Sitting here as though nothing was up!"

"Well, Yekel," one of the boys sat down next to the old man. "Getting ready for a true feast?"

"Too early!" The old man's scraggly beard shook. As the boys crowded around him, he held out his two palms, like scales, in mock consternation. "What's all the to-do? Where's the hurry?"

"We have to greet the bride and groom properly!"

"Ride out on horseback to greet them!"

"The whole company!"

"Is that so?" The sexton plunged a finger into a huge rip in a boy's coat. "With these royal garments you can go on foot—you don't need horses."

"We're changing our clothing, Grandpa!"

"We're going in disguise!"

"With swords!"

"In armor!"

"True knights!"

"And I, Yekel, am Prince Bova," a lad said,

striking a pose. He was as long and lean as a post marking the Sabbath boundary.

Next to the lanky boy suddenly sprang up a short fellow, round as a drum. Running his fingers down his friend's long back, as though plucking the strings of a harp, he burst into song:

"Ne'er, ne'er in all my life
Have I beheld so valiant a knight.
Why look ye at this strutting cock
That needs must battle round the clock.
I wean, 'tis Dietrich of Berne, with his mighty
sword,
Or Hildebrandt, or some other renowned
lord!"

Laughing fit to burst at the comical antics of the yeshiva boys, Daniel flung himself into a series of cartwheels; next he spun like a top all over the courtyard, the spectacular display of his youthful prowess ending with a long "Whee—ee-ee."

"And where is the beauteous damsel Drusiana?" someone asked.

"You mean darling Sarah, the headmaster's daughter?" winked the fat boy.

"Heaven forfend that I should taste the dainty bridal flesh!"

"Heaven forfend that I should choke on her!"

"She looks like a flat cake!"

"Pooh, this is nasty talk!" The sexton shooed the yeshiva boys away, like a flock of birds.

A boy with a hunched back and no neck stepped forward.

"And I, Yekel, am Joab, the son of Zeruiah."

"And I, gentleman, am David, King of Israel,"
bowed a boy with flaming hair and red earlocks.

Drum-belly fell to singing again:

*"David stripped the giant of
His harness, sword, and spear.
Quoth he: I'll sell it all in town—
'Twill bring me in a thousand crown—
All this useless gear!"*

"And you, roly-poly, are always playing the
clown!" exclaimed the sexton to the crowd, pointing
disparagingly. "He can recite, that one, he has the
real gift of speech."

"And there's something else he can do, too,
Yekel!"

Moshel of Cracow, a fifty-year-old superannuated yeshiva "boy," who had been to every yeshiva
in Ashkenaz and France, thrust himself forward
with the self-important air of one about to read the
prayers before the Holy Ark:

"And I, gentlemen, am Master Hildebrandt
himself!"

"A lie, a lie! The Gentile Hildebrandt observed the ban of Rabbi Gershom! He never es-
poused more than one wife at a time!"

"And I?" Moshel goggled like a simpleton who
could not count past two.

"You?" cried several lads at once. "You're always available! At every yeshiva, you're in the espousal business!"

"Moshel," one of the boys pointed to two lice
strolling underneath Moshel's collar, "you are a
caitiff knight-errant!"

"Nothing but nasty talk!" The sexton pulled a small book out of his pocket. He held it close to his eyes. "What doth Rabbi Yuda the Pious teach us? Yes, here it is. 'If thou shouldst observe a louse on thy fellow's garment, accuse him not before a stranger's eyes: shame not thy fellow, for that is sinful.' "

"These are a plague one can't escape, dear Yekel," smiled middle-aged Moshel. "I conjure them with oaths, I anathematize them, I banish them with all kinds of permutations and combinations of the Divine Name—but nought avails! You lie down to sleep and they carry you out of your bed. The very straw heaves to their tramp, tramp, tramp!"

"We've delivered funeral orations over their graves but nought avails!"

"May the marriage be in a lucky hour!" someone cried, clapping his hands.

"For the bride's family, and for the groom's!"

"Look, here come the honest-to-goodness in-laws!"

"That's not the in-laws—'tis a cloudburst! God be with us!"

From all sides the synagogue was invaded by a legion of beggars—limping, lame, blind, humps on their backs and humps on their chests. They came with their wives, their children, their packs. With a rat-tat-tat of peg legs and walking sticks and flaying hooks, they spread through the synagogue courtyard like an excrescence, young and old thundering all at once:

"We're starved to death!"

"We've had nothing but bad luck!"
"Where is the espousal house?"
"There's a good meal due us!"
"With meat!"
"Where's that sexton?"
"There he sits, outside!"

At sight of the beggars, the yeshiva students forgot the fine dinner waiting for them, forgot the wives and children waiting for them somewhere in Ashkenaz, forgot the comfortable rabbinical posts waiting in their futures.

Full of mortal danger and uncertainty, the roads that led abroad stretched alluringly before their mind's eye. They could not sit still; there were learned "innovations" to carry into every corner of their known world, together with the profane "romances" in their packs. However little or great their learning, driven by a longing for freedom they would wander from Poland to Ashkenaz, from Ashkenaz to Italy, thence to France, where they could at long last loosen the restrictions that generations had fastened on their gaunt bodies.

II

The synagogue courtyard turned black with the companies of beggars that descended on the earth like crows. The air was loud with voices—long-drawn-out and choppy—whose sound fell on the ear like the screeching of storks flying home in the spring.

Three beggar-chiefs pushed forward and looked about for a fourth. First came a man who had lost an eye; the second had a beer-barrel paunch; the third, a twisted mouth. They yelled for red-headed Sender.

"Hey, Red!"

"Where have you disappeared to?"

Sender's red beard, glowing in the sun, flamed in a circle around his open mouth and lapped his tanned cheeks. As he strode vigorously forward in his wrinkled boots, his fathom-wide shoulders, capable of lifting up a wagon-load, evoked respect.

"Here I am!"

The four set out for the watchroom, where sexton Berl was sitting with his father, waiting to take down the beggars' names and places of origin.

"Sholom aleichem, Master Yekel, peace be with you, Master Berl!" the four beggar-chiefs cried in unison; the salutation rang like an oath.

"Aleichem sholom, with you be peace," Yekel intoned the traditional response, his white beard nodding. Had not his son been present, he would have given each of the newcomers his hand in greeting.

For Yekel, who never in his life had set foot out of Regensburg, never made light of beggars. To the contrary: he was powerfully attracted to these venturesome fellows who moved to and fro across God's earth. They were familiar with all manner of men; it was said that their travels took them to the very edge of the sacred river Sambatyon, behind

which live the Lost Ten Tribes of Israel. They always had much to recount.

But Berl did not reply to the beggar's "Sholom
Aleichem." Chasing little Daniel away, he fixed his
eyes suspiciously on the hustlers' nimble fingers
and asked angrily:

"You are the chiefs?"

All four shook their beards in the affirmative.

"How many of you are there?"

"Over a hundred."

"Tell me exactly, it has to be put down."

"One hundred and five—damn the plague! Is
that enough for you?"

"More than enough, more than enough." Berl's
beard jutted defiantly. "But don't you play games
with me! How many *of your kind* are there?"

"We haven't had a chance to catch our breath."
The one-eyed fellow stepped forward. "Nought to
eat, nought to drink, and you start in on us, Master
Berl. Why are you so wroth?"

"That's the truth, why all the wrath, Master
Berl? You're not a so-and-so like the Worms servitor," Crooked Mouth blurted out. He grabbed his
fellow-chief with the big belly. "Well, Hershele, how
go things? Tell me the world isn't all topsy-turvy!
True, we're beggars, but when that Worms servitor
started up with us—what happened, Hershele? Tell
him!"

Hershele didn't wait for a second invitation.
Crossing his short arms on his immense belly, he
shut his eyes and remained stock still for a moment,

as if carved of stone. Then he fell to singing in a
voice that issued from deep in his belly:

"Hearken to me, O all ye dear folk
That languish in this world so wide
When we at Worms-town did arrive—
Oh, what a world this is, dear folk!

"Invited guests, we marched into Worms
But they closed the doors upon us:
Then up strode the servitor of Worms
And brandished his stick agin' us,

"One by one to the watchroom he hails us.
'How long doth thou stay? And what art thou
called?'
And with such questioning assails us
That wormy servitor of Worms!"

"That's enough, enough!" Yekel put his hands
over his ears.

"Let him finish, Father."

"Yes, please let him finish, Grandpa," pleaded
little Daniel.

"No, no," the old man clutched Hershel's coat.
"How can a Jew indulge in such filth? First *you* talk
against the servitor, then the servitor talks against
you, and between the both of you the Name of God
is profaned."

Hershel danced about the old sexton.

"And is it nought, you say, that the Worms
councilors, all of them, the parness included, do
abuse poor folk—that is nought, you say?"

"Listen to me, fellow-Jews," pleaded the old man, "go along quietly to the dance house."

"We're going, we're going! But tell us, if you don't mind, where are we to eat?"

"In the bakery in the dance house cellar, where tables have been set for you."

"And what news of the jesters?" Red Beard inquired, as a kind of afterthought.

"Nought's been heard or seen of them as yet." Berl went to the corner of the watchroom for some sand to dry what he had written.

Red Sender followed, and whispered in his ear: "If 'tis needful, we can do anything."

"What things can you do?" Berl spread the sand over the ink with two fingers.

"Anything and everything—we can play the flute, walk on stilts, sing and recite, swallow snakes, juggle beer and wine flasks, play pranks—as good and better than professional jesters! Just say the word, and we'll pull our bag of tricks out of our sleeves!"

"It will have to be fifty-fifty," Berl straightened up, and his cleft, swallow-tail beard jutted at the hustlers.

"Our word for it!"

"And do you have something special for the lasses?"

"We've a new song that will quicken their spirits: 'Where They Sleep All Four.'" Red Beard laid his hands on his bare, hairy chest. "Hershele! Where the devil is he? Hershele! Let's have that song, the one where the lass flings the rogue out the window!"

As though he had been waiting for the word of command, Hershel threw his head back, and took a deep breath that swelled his beer-barrel belly to immense proportions. Assuming a piteous expression, he began pleading with some invisible person standing in the corner of the watchroom:

"I came before my dear love's door—
The door was bolted tight.
O dear love, dear love, let me in,
Lest I freeze, tonight.

"Yes, I shall let thee in
Lest thou freeze tonight."

Hershele sang on, in fine voice, stanza after stanza. He was at the very climax of the tale, where the rogue refuses to remain true to his dear love and the lass binds him hand and foot and flings him out the window.

Suddenly, the words stuck in Hershele's gullet. There at the door stood the head of the yeshiva, a tall man wearing a black garment that buttoned at the neck, like a woman's cloak.

"What's this—ballads! Jester's ribaldry and abomination in the synagogue courtyard? So a rich man's having a wedding—well, what of that? Does that mean everything's permissible? Off with you, off to the dance house! Sing your harlot's songs again, and out of the city you march! And you, Yekel—a decent old Jew like you, to sit and listen to such ribaldry!"

Yekel and his son rose guiltily before the head of the yeshiva. Little Daniel hid under the table.

The four beggars shuffled to the door. But Red Beard's eyes were burning, his nostrils flaring. One leap would carry him to the throat of his ancient enemy, the head of the yeshiva.

"People need luck in all things, even in the poor God sends them," said the old sexton to the head of the yeshiva. "What says Rabbi Yuda the Pious? 'We must ever beg the good Lord to send us decent poor folk.' "

"But you have forgotten, Yekel," said the head of the yeshiva, somewhat mollified. "Rabbi Yuda the Pious also said: 'Take no joy in Gentile dancing and prancing, fencing and tourneying, and you shall be found worthy to rejoice in the feast of the Leviathan!' "

"Golden words, Master," the old man nodded.

"But we are no Gentiles," the broad-shouldered beggar-chief mumbled nasally, imitating the outlandish speech of the Spanish-born head of the yeshiva, whose accent was was that of neither Jew nor Gentile.

"You're worse than Gentiles!" shouted Berl. "As for you, Red Cutpurse—take to your heels!"

"But wasn't it you," the beggar-chief thrust out his hairy chest, "weren't you the one so anxious to go partners with this 'worse-than-a-Gentile?' "

"I?" Berl prepared to hurl himself at Red Beard, who could nonchalantly have rolled the young sexton up into a ball and shoved him into the sack that hung over his right shoulder.

Before Yekel and the head of the yeshiva could move to separate the two mismatched combatants, the synagogue courtyard shook to the loud music of the flute, the sound of dancing and the jangling of bells. A personage with a peg leg hobbled into the watchroom.

"Mazel Tov! Good luck! The Prague jesters have arrived!"

Red Beard lightly brushed the young sexton out of his way. His thievish eyes gleamed at his fellows, who stood still, taken aback.

"What are you standing about for, whoremongers?"

The beggars rushed through the door like a wind; the next moment the door reopened. First Hershel's potbelly appeared, then his open maw with what seemed to be a hundred teeth:

> *"We beg by night, we beg by day*
> *May the devil take you all away!"*

"Wretch!"

"Rapscallion!"

"I'll have him arrested straight away!" cried the head of the yeshiva, whose shoulders were bent from study, like a well-pole under buckets of water. Nervously, his long white fingers twisted his collar button, as he repeated rapidly. "I'll have him arrested at once, the cutpurse!"

Delighted at the furor, little Daniel crept out from under the table and did a handstand. Unobserved he stuck out a small red tongue at the head of the yeshiva. Then he stared at his father. Berl was struggling to break free from Yekel's hands, shouting:

"Let me go, Father, let me at him! I'll slay him, the rascal, I'll trample him to the dirt! The beggar! Let me go, Father, let me go!" But with all his protestations, he made no attempt to move from the spot.

III

The covered wagon with its harnessed horses stood in the middle of the synagogue courtyard. The cloth covers were tied back and the flute and jew's harp incessantly proclaimed the tidings of the arrival of the jesters from Prague.

A crowd quickly gathered, spilling out of the houses and the narrow courtyards. Here and there, small windows were opened. Young and old, men and women, leaned out over the sills, resting on their stomachs and elbows, to stare with fascination at the synagogue courtyard; down below, the concourse was so dense the wagon was almost invisible.

The sound of the flute and the drum blared out in the hot afternoon air. One by one, the beggars, who had welcomed the jesters with curses and threats, grew silent. They forgot about the meat meal that awaited then in the dance house. Throwing off their packs, they sprawled out near the synagogue walls and steps, and around the cool stone well, scaring off a flock of sparrows bathing in the sand.

Benignly, the sun shone down upon the beggars, warming their chill bones, baking the vermin from off their hairy bodies, tangled beards, and louse-ridden heads.

In the midst of the jesters strolled a sunburned girl, her dark eyes wild and restless. Small, firm breasts pushed forth like hillocks under the bodice of her short, tight-fitting dress, which flared out at the knees with pleats, ruffles, and pockets. Her slim, nimble feet, cased in slippers with bells, tapped even when she was still.

"There's a firebrand for you!" the yeshiva boy with red earlocks pointed to the wagon.

"I'd love to be lying with her tonight," Moshele Cracower smiled in his beard. "A delicious tidbit, fit for a king."

"You would only nibble, only tickle, like a kinglet."

"Which is what women prefer." Moshele elbowed his way toward the wagon. "And you, Saint Zalman, you are staring at the lass with your mouth open as though a roast dove had fallen into it!"

"Off with you and your filthy mouth," Zalman reprimanded the superannuated student. "Tell me: who is that elongated palm branch dancing attendance on her?"

"I gather, from his dress and gait, he's a stilt-walker."

"Moshel, I've an idea." Zalman felt his breast pocket, to make sure his opus *Amnon and Tamar* was still there. "Perhaps here's a chance for business. What do you say to our having a little talk with the jesters about my song-play—and getting to see that pretty little dancer at the same time?"

"Now you are thinking!" Moshel was delighted. "It's the blessed Lord who sent you a 'Tamar' with bells on for the occasion!"

The stilt-walker, a tall, thin man, hopped down from the wagon. He passed through the crowd pleading:

"Masters! Make room for us, masters!"

The crowd opened up to form a semi-circle around the wagon. The stilt-walker good-humoredly lifted his long stork legs. His jester's face was distended in an expression of rascally trickery. His thin, drawn lips whistled replies to the crowd's questions:

"What are we here to do?
To sing and laugh for you.
Laugh and sing for you.
That's why we have come—
To make things hum!"

"Zalman," Moshel whispered to his comrade, "if all goes well, I have a foot in the jesters' door."

"Tell me about it!"

"You see that fellow over there?"

"The one holding a goat mask in his hand?"

"He and I were school chums, studied together under Rabbi Leibush of Prague. You have to go far to find another such prankster. 'Pon my word, it is him—Fishel, the tosspot!"

"Should I call to him?"

"Wait a moment. You've got that pretty thing on your mind. If it really is Fishel, I'd not like to become the butt of his sharp tongue. In Prague everyone shivered when he opened his mouth, even the head of the yeshiva. And when Fishel set about mocking the women at the Hanukkah and Purim plays, it was sheer impudence and scandal! Their ears fairly burned with shame and humiliation—and yet, despite everything, the women loved him for it, even slept with him, that brazen creature."

"The Talmud says in the tractate *Sotah*," Zalman cried happily, "Every woman desireth a measure of frivolity."

Making a sudden leap, all at once the stilt-walker sprang up onto the floor of the open wagon. He stretched until he was a head taller. A sharp curving nose stood out on his longish face like the beak of a predatory bird. With mincing steps he walked twice to and fro over the wagon floor. Then, as the synagogue courtyard grew quiet, he turned to face the jesters. His long, narrow hands hung limp at his sides, as he both sang and whistled:

> *"Tell me comrades, masters,*
> *What kind of folk are ye?"*

Some dozen mouths opened wide and the synagogue courtyard rang with the reply. The dancer's voice piped high above the men's voices, as the jesters' reply resounded above the heads of the audience.

> *"Ah yes, an' yes, an' yes,*
> *We sing and we play,*
> *We dance and sport the livelong day—*
> *Brave folk is what we are.*
> *Brave folk are we!"*

The stilt-walker moved to a corner of the wagon; his voice and long beard inquired:

*"Don't you hail from Prague,
From the scholar's side?"*

The jesters rocked around the dancer. She clapped her hands, tapped her feet; her eyes, deep and dark, flickered with stormy flames:

*"Ah yes, an' yes, an' yes,
We hail from Prague, we do,
From the scholar's side.
We are jesters out of Prague,
Brave folk is what we are.
Brave folk are we.*

*"Ah yes, an' yes, an' yes,
We are jesters out of Prague—
Tralalalalala."*

The crowd, which had joined in the response, fell back, making room for the dancer, who ran among them with outstretched tambourine. She laughed with her white teeth, with her eyes, with her oval face, smooth as dark olives. From every side coins flew into the tambourine.

"What's the dancer's name?"

"Rosa is my name, throw your coins into the tambourine, throw them in my hand; it is all the same, I will understand." The dancer's eyes sparkled. Even the most staid householders smiled in their beards, their round-brimmed hats shaking with delight.

"Rosalein, sing us the song: 'In Austria a Castle Stands.'"

"Too tired, too tired, masters." Rosa flung

back her head; her heavy black braids trailed on her graceful shoulders. "After the marriage, I'll sing to harps and flutes, fiddles and drums."

The smell of freshly baked ginger and of sugared almond cookies assailed them. It was followed by the smells of stewed goose and beet soup and thimble-dumplings. Faint with hunger, the jesters languished at the delicious odors.

Chayim the baker arrived, covered all over with flour, as though he too had just been taken out of the oven. After him, two apprentices hurried up with tins of fresh baked meats for Master Samuel Belasser's wedding.

The baker caught sight of the dancer and stood stock still. The apprentices peered at their master thievishly.

"What good things have you here?" The dancer was at the baker's side, her delicate, small hand laid on his. "Won't you treat a hungry dancing girl?"

"The best and the most beautiful!" The baker circled the dancer, taking her around the waist with delight. "Come, my pretty actor-girl, shall we leave the bride and groom for a while and have ourselves a good time?"

The apprentices squatted; they crouched with lowered heads. The dancer stuffed handfuls of cookies and dumplings into the pockets and pleats of her skirt. An almond cookie crumbled under her sharp teeth; her little tongue dexterously licked crumbs from her lips.

"Chayim, do the Jew dance!" someone
clapped.

"The Jew dance, Chayim!"

"What, here in the synagogue courtyard?"
chided an elderly Jewess. But no one paid her any
heed.

Rosa raised her tambourine. Her firm breasts
fluttered under her tight dress like palpitating birds.
She stepped back, one foot keeping time. The bells
on her bodice and the bells on her skirt tinkled, and
the tinkling set the crowd's feet going. One of her
braids, loosened by the movement of her head,
swung in the air before her. Rosa's every movement, every turn, sang with her:

"A fair young wife am I
And have an ancient hubby.
Snow-white is my body, O,
But no one ever sees it."

Beside himself, the baker slapped his thighs,
and a cloud of flour flew into his eyes. He ran after
the dancer, who artfully escaped his outstretched
arms. Bursting with laughter, the crowd derided the
baker:

"Chayim, what do you plan on baking? White
Sabbath twists?"

"Almond cookies?"

"You have to know how to dance, Chayim!"

The baker lads, with the tins of bake-meats still
on their heads, squatting on their broad haunches,
moved their shoulders in rhythm. An elderly beggar
woman sprang forward from the edge of the crowd.

She raised her ragged dress with both hands; naked, unspeakably filthy legs burlesqued Rosa's dance.

When finally the dancer permitted the baker to catch her, he was all out of breath, and pale as a ghost. Every one joined in the song with Rosa, tapping their feet and clapping:

> *"A fair young wife am I*
> *And have an ancient hubby...."*

IV

The dancer stopped singing. She drew two fingers across her loose braid like a bow across a violin, curtsied briefly to the crowd, and jangled her bells. She remained standing on one leg, and every movement of her lithe body was like the crack of a whip. Her even teeth flashed in her small mouth. Her glance swept from face to face through the crowd with such intensity that they held their sides in laughter. Cries rose from their open mouths:

"Rosalein!"

"Hurrah Rosalein! Hurrah!"

The older and more respectable householders, like shamefaced boys, hid their laughter in their beards and in the bellies, big and small, that protruded from their broad jackets and short, tight coats. Walking with slow and measured steps, they went each his separate way, one into a house, another into a side street. Vastly amused, they left the jesters behind, as though seeking shelter from a sun shower whose droplets glisten under the sun's rays.

In the open wagon someone strummed a jew's harp. The drum played accompaniment. The rhythm crackled like chestnuts in a copper frying pan.

"Where is that Fishel of yours?" Zalman demanded of Moshel.

"He has disappeared." Moshel's head turned this way and that, as his eyes sought Fishel in the covered wagon.

The goat mask still in his hand, Fishel had crept into the back of the wagon. He threw the mask among the packed barrels and sacks, and stood in a corner, depressed. The pretense of jollity melted from his face; pain and hurt lay in his restless eyes and tight-knit mouth. He shuddered and gritted his teeth; the shouting and hurrahing of the crowd was intolerable to him.

That's all they cared for—song and laughter, laughter and song. It was he, Fishel who composed the elaborate harangues, the madcap pranks, the songs, the verse plays—but the others who performed them, were skimming off the cream of the glory. That he had lived to see this day! It used to be that when a parness or rich man had a wedding, he would call on Fishel first. When the local Gentile gentry were invited, the princes and counts, Fishel could always be counted on to loosen his facile tongue. He would offer them a "romance," a pretty song or two, some sayings in the priestly Latin tongue. The "lords and masters" would perk up their ears and, lifting beakers of wine, would sing along with Fishel, "setting the brass platters on the wall a-rattle."

"Vivat, long life to the player!"

"Hurrah! Vivat!"

But nowadays? Nowadays, it was "short on talk and long on action." The vulgar had no appreciation of the finer things. It was always "Rosalein! Rosalein! Vivat Rosalein!"

Fishel parted the cloth hanging over the back of the wagon and lightly slipped down into the courtyard. Pulling his pointed cap down over his forehead after the rapscallion fashion, he whistled softly. He had a yen to catch a glimpse of what was happening at Belasser's. That was a home where you could still find an appreciative ear for a keen morsel of peppery dialectic, even if it were slightly off-color. The company of jesters had simply become intolerable to him.

Fishel was short of stature. His pale face was framed by a small black beard, heavy around the chin, but sparse, almost bare, on the cheeks. Fishel's nervous hands seemed always to be engaged in a conversation with one another. His eyes were hungry, piercing; they darted about as he sought a path through the horde of beggars. But he could not help casting an occasional glance at the crowd, which was by now past the stage of laughter, and had gone wild with merrymaking.

Fishel was completely out of sorts. Now nothing pleased him—neither the blinding, hot afternoon, nor the crowd's high spirits—no, not even the prospect of the wedding.

Not knowing what to do with himself, he circled about the synagogue courtyard alone. What was it that gnawed at his heart: hunger or melancholy? Whichever it was, life tasted bitter.

"Where shall I go from here?" He stopped and stood with open palms, as though to balance the choices before him. "Exchange the jester's cap for an ordinary hat and attend the Regensburg yeshiva?"

Unconsciously, at the thought of the yeshiva, his lips recited the words he had composed about the Prague penitent. A smile formed on his small, carelessly trimmed beard:

> "Lo amut, *I shall not die, I wish to live and love,*
> *To give all honor to the Blessed Name above.*"

A packman appeared from the direction of Jew Street—a full-fleshed personage, big as a "long summer Friday." His beard, of which you could count every hair, was yellow; his short, thick earlocks were blond; his cheeks, red. His blue, kindly eyes seemed incongruous with the rest of his body, which resembled that of a Hollander rather than a Jew.

First off, the packman set down a knobby stick, whose broad top was shaped like a seat, so that he could sit on it. He removed the arm bands from his shoulders, and slipped the pack off his back; even before he had spread out his books, a crowd began to collect.

The packman was a stranger, and yet a figure perfectly at home in Regensburg. Alien, he traveled from country to country, had been all over the world, had seen everything, heard everything. Though you sat with him listening for a year and a day, you could still not exhaust his treasury of stories. Packmen arrived in Ashkenaz in the summertime together with the migratory birds returning home. Dispersing the winter sadness, they recounted how fellow-Jews lived in Stamboul, in Palestine, and even in the lands behind the Dark Mountains.

Fishel regarded the full-fleshed personage and was delighted.

The bookseller wiped the huge mustachios concealing his mouth, and sang out:

"Brand new! Brand new! Come running to my stall, come running one and all! A fine prayer book, together with an up-to-date translation! Not only for pious wives and maidens,—but for young men too, and for husbands—don't be dismayed! Here's something for every Jew, be he man or wife, so long as he can read aright. Masters and mistresses, I deem ignoramuses those who hear the words of the Holy Tongue, but understand not a single one!"

"Very well sermonized," a Jew prodded his neighbor. "There's a tongue no healer need shorten!"

"I envy no one an encounter with him in the dark!"

"What a face for a Jew to be wearing!"

"They're not content printing 'romances' in the spoken tongue." The Regensburg slaughterer leafed through a prayer book with the honed index fingernail he used to test the sharpness of his knives. "Now they're also printing prayers in the common language. Who needs it?"

"Where did you say this was printed?" a customer showed the bookseller an open prayer book. "There's no sign of where the press is."

"Where the press is?" The bookseller's blue eyes fell to laughing. "You understand, nuncle, the press is where I press it, and that is where I am pressed. As for me, I am known to fame; Joseph Tannhauser's son is my name."

"Why are you wasting your time gabbing with scholars?" an elderly Jewess clutched the bookseller's sleeve. "People like that won't buy your merchandise anyway! But I appreciate you! You have earned your share in the hereafter! Every matron who can read and buys your prayer book can become an honest-to-goodness cantor; she need not merely be an 'out-loud reader' for the illiterates. We'll no longer need tap on the pane of the woman's section to ask the menfolk, 'Where are you up to in the service? Where d'ye hold?' And what would be the price of this prayer book of yours?"

The bookseller paid almost no heed to the Jewess. He had his eye on the crowd fingering his merchandise, for he knew full well that even a holy prayer book was not beyond pilferage. With one eye on the Jewess, he sang out his packman's chant:

"Here's a prayer book for all year round, 'tis well translated, true and sound. So come and buy, ladies and misses, don't you pass this prayer book by. Books like these don't grow on trees, they're bound to instruct and bound to please. 'Tis not too much for any purse, one crown buys it, to read and rehearse!"

"Too dear! Too dear!"

"What is it—a precious stone? A jewel?"

"There is a glut of this merchandise—God preserve us!"

"Can be gotten at half the price!"

"Did you hear that? A whole crown!"

"One crown too dear?" The bookseller laughed so heartily his beard shook. "This prayer book would be a find at ten. Compare it with any other—'tis as different as an old jade is from a fresh lass!"

"Well done! Well said!" Fishel pointed to the prayer book. "Here's a lass one needn't bother to sin with!"

"That's sacrilege!" The packman regarded Fishel's garb.

"He's one of the jesters," a voice from the crowd called out.

"If that's the case," the bookseller wiped his hand on his beard, "I have special merchandise for you—Italian ware. But you have to be a connoisseur to appreciate it." He pulled a pamphlet of sewn pages, not yet covered, out of a side pocket.

"Look at this script! 'Twill brighten your eyes! There's no broken or heavy type can compare with this script! You know who it was that wrote it? Gimpel the scribe, no lesser person—a master whom the world acclaims."

"I know him."

"And do you know Gimpel's brother-in-law, Elijah Bochur, who turned the Italian Bova Book into Yiddish?"

"Of course, Elijah is in Venice now." Fishel grew more cordial. "His father, Asher of Ipsheim, taught me Hebrew grammar, and his mother, Hindlin—there's no prankster her match for a hundred furlongs around Nuremberg!"

"Since you know the whole famliy, perhaps this is ware more to your taste!" The packman pulled out still another pamphlet and handed it to Fishel.

Fishel intoned:

"A marvelous tale of the doings in King Arthur's court, of tourneys, dalliance and sport, and of the famous knight Sir Gawain, he that fought with might and main, in rhyme both elegant and plain."

"I have two manuscript copies of this," Fishel returned the *Tales of King Arthur's Court*.

Moshel Cracower arrived, with Zalman at his heels. Taking Fishel by the shoulder, Moshel regarded him roguishly, his eyes flashing, yet uncertain of his former comrade's reception: "Fishel, don't you remember your old friend anymore?"

"Why, it's Moshel!" Fishel spun the fifty-year-old yeshiva student about like a top. The crowd roared with delight. "Still a virgin, my lad? Come here, Moshel, give me your hand, give me your kiss! Damn, are you bashful?" Fishel pointed to a girl standing nearby with a bevy of friends. "I'll kiss her instead!"

The girls put their hands over their mouths,

huddled together like lambs and, choking on their giggles, fled across the street.

"Still having fun, eh Fishel?" Moshel was vastly pleased to be recognized. In his mind he was going over the names of all the yeshivas which they had attended.

"Yes, I'm still a connoisseur when it comes to a fine wench or an honest quaff." Fishel looked around him, to make sure he had not lost his audience. "Is there a tavern in this town where a man can quench a thirst?"

"Michel's Golden Deer is the place for you." Moshel pulled Zalman forward; the latter was on tenterhooks. "Let me introduce a friend: this is Zalman—he writes playlets full of pepper and ginger."

"Comrade is the proper word." Fishel shook hands with the lad, and was delighted to see him blush like a girl.

"What tidings do I have to report?" Moshel grasped his beard, as though contemplating a difficult passage in the Talmud. "Our own Leib of Regensburg has composed a new work, called *Tales of King David's Court.*"

"Leib—you mean that wretch, that sot?" Fishel immediately flew into rage. "Even if he were the incarnation of Samuel the Singer, or Cosi, or Caphan, he could never write anything half as good as *Dietrich of Berne* or *Apprentice Hildebrandt,* or that wondrous lovely and melancholy tale, *King Sigmund and His Beloved Magdelene.* Leib's writings please no one but pious old women and tale-mongers!"

Moshel lowered his voice and spoke very low and fast.

"Good or bad, the head of the yeshiva told me that only pious tales will be sung and recited at Belasser's wedding." This was something for Fishel's ears only—the Regensburg citizens were not meant to hear. "The head of the yeshiva said explicitly that there was to be no *Dietrich of Berne* or *Pretty Glick* at the espousals—none of that 'filth and abomination.' "

"That's a lie! Falsehood and defamation!" Fishel clenched his fists. "Who is the head of your yeshiva?"

"The author of *Shield of David*."

"That Sephardi? Why, he speaks Yiddish like a Gentile! I know him well, I know him from way back, from the old days in Prague! Yes, and I know his famous lineage too—he is a descendent of the renowned Nachmanides." Fishel shook his head in anger. "I swear, these Sephardim despise everything about us Ashkenazim, including our language! Inflated peacocks! As for me, I maintain that any one of our saintly rabbis is a finer and a better Jew than all their learned scholars put together!"

"That's what I say," interjected Zalman. "They think everything has to give way to their 'philosophy.' I don't know which the academy head respects more—the Doctrine of Aristotle, or the Torah of Moses. For my part, the Ashkenazi Rashi is more important than all those fancy scholars."

"He's all right, that lad of yours! Bless him, he's got a head on his shoulders." Fishel chucked Zalman under the chin. "One would judge from your accent that you are a 'Hittite'; from Vienna perhaps, or from Neustadt?"

"Why a Hittite?" Zalman smiled.

"You can't hide from me. I can recognize a Neustadter even when he keeps his mouth closed. Come on, now, let's hear you say 'Opmekken.' "*

"Opmekhken."

All three of them laughed goodnaturedly.

Moshel was encouraged by Fishel's familiarity with Zalman. "My comrade Zalman has a bit of merchandise for your inspection. He has written a song-play fit for a king."

"And he says nary a word, the rascal!" Fishel cried, tickling Moshel between the ribs. "What's it called?"

"*Amnon and Tamar,*" Zalman replied breathlessly.

"Do you have it with you?"

"Yes."

"Then let's away to the tavern. Away! But wait," Fishel turned back to the wagon and both whistled and shouted: "Rosa! Ro-sa!"

"Coming, coming!" the dancer came running up.

"First of all, the introductions," Fishel cried in high spirits. "Two comrades—Rosa. Rosa—two

* The Yiddish word *Opmekken,* "to erase," could conceivably have derived from the German *ab* (from) and the Hebrew *maḥok* (to rub off).

comrades. Now, Rosa, we must use our heads. This lad has written a play. It's called *Amnon and Tamar*. Let's all repair to the tavern for liquid refreshments—he'll read it to us there. Come along, my Tamar."

"I take the author," Rosa joined Zalman.

"You like him?"

"I do!" The dancer slipped her arm into Zalman's.

"Now Rosa, none of your brazen ways," Fishel whispered into Rosa's ear. "Leave the lad alone, or they'll expel him from Regensburg."

"Just to make you burst with envy, I'm going with him!" laughed Rosa, embracing Zalman in the middle of the street.

Zalman slipped out of Rosa's arms. Looking around, he encountered large black eyes fixed on him, and his face blanched, his earlocks flaming all the more.

Near the Ghetto portico a woman in black was leaning out of a window. The visible upper half of her body seemed to be growing out of the triangular sign fixed to the wall.

Fishel read the legend aloud:

MADAME LOPEZ

DOCTOR OF THE FREE PROFESSION

PHYSICIAN

IN RESIDENCE AT REGENSBURG

He bowed: "I, madame physician, am a jester, and this pretty personage (pointing to Rosa) is an actress."

"And the lad with the red earlocks?" The lady physician shook the amber earrings that fell to her shoulders.

"The lad?" Fishel smiled. "He is looking for magic specifics, roots, and mushrooms."

"What, would he win the actor-girl through means of magic?"

"Yes, my precious madame physician."

"He will never win her that way," Rosa winked.

"Right and true, actor-girl, right and true," the lady physician burst into laughter. "And where do you lodge tonight?"

"Under the open sky," Fishel lifted his eyes to heaven.

"I have lodgings for two or three."

"Thank you, we thank you from the depths of our hearts," Fishel bowed profoundly. "And now let us leave the good madame physician and away to the tavern."

V

At the Golden Deer, hard by the Jew Street gate, the air throbbed with the strong smell of beer, whisky and wine. Three slippery steps led down to the tavern in the cellar. In the damp, dark vestibule, Fishel took Moshel Cracower aside. Slipping his arm around his old schoolmate's thick waist, he said: "O my sworn brother-in-drink, my nose tells me that this is a place where a man can get a goodly pitcher of ale. Tell me, comrade, do you happen to have an extra reichsthaler on your person? As for me, God preserve me, I am a pretty pauper!"

"And I, brother mine, am a still prettier one!" Moshel spread his elbows like bat wings in the darkness. His pockets were empty.

"No coins, comrades? Trust me—I'll see to it." The dancer ran down the steps to the door, which she opened impetuously—only to recoil, as though she had banged into a drum.

In the open door stood a tall, thin personage, his lips red and fleshy, his beard and eyes black as a thief's.

"What's the to-do? Where are you running?" Angrily the man stepped back from the door and measured the newcomers with a glance so hard that they all retreated.

The stranger's dark eyes frowned at Moshel. But as they settled on the dancer, his anger evaporated. Instinctively, he felt his bulging pockets. Then, pointing a finger at Moshel Cracower, he asked:

"Who is she? The actor-girl from Prague?"

"You guessed right, Sachse," Moshel said flatteringly; he liked to be of service to wealthy men.

"And who is he?" Sachse pointed to Fishel but kept his eyes on the dancer. "He has the appearance of a wandering minstrel or jester."

"You are right again." Moshel took Fishel aside and whispered into his ear. "Sachse traffics in precious stones. Look at his pockets—they are stuffed with jewelry. Rich as Korah, and a great fancier of the lasses."

"Well then, since you have guessed that I am a wandering minstrel," Fishel thrust his head into the rich man's face, with all the bravado of the jester, "promise me, by mouth and by hand, to listen to a peppery dialectic composed by a poor wandering minstrel, who needs a drink and hasn't a penny to his name."

"No preliminaries, jester, no preliminaries." The rich Regensburger saw a jest at his expense in the offing. "Where is your bit of pilpulistic* by-play?"

Fishel tugged at his pointed cap, extended his hands in opposite directions and asked:

"Which kind of pilpul do you prefer—the Regensburg kind, or the Nuremberg?"

"The Regensburg—by all means!"

"There is an explicit text in the Talmud," began Fishel. "To wit: Purim is a holiday. At which the sages of Regensburg rise, take their stand, and pose their profound question, to wit: Seeing as Purim is a holiday, and Rabbi Judah the pious has ruled that the recital of the Kiddush prayer sanctifying the day is obligatory on every holiday, and seeing as the Kiddush can only be recited over wine— well then, where does Pauper Dalfon secure the wine for Kiddush? Ah, but suppose a jester from Prague appears and makes answer that Pauper Dalfon must borrow the money for the wine, for the Kiddush, for the holy day of Purim, why then, the same iron-clad question remains: What idiot would lend money to a pauper? Along comes Rabbi Drop,

* *Pilpul* means "pepper," and is also applied to sharp-witted talmudic argumentation.

may his reward be sorrow and sighing, and makes answer, to wit: Purim is ever a holiday. As to what manner of idiot would lend money for wine? The answer is Dalfon's brother Vaisasa!"*

"What are we drinking, beer?" Rosa interrupted Fishel, hugging him so hard he lost the breath to finish his pilpul.

"The drinks are on me today," the Regensburg Maecenas shouted to the innkeeper. "Michel, two pitchers of sour wine and one of sweet—immediately!"

"And something to eat, too!" Rosa laughed into Sachse's face. Overwhelmed with delight, he offered the dancer a bracelet.

But Zalman was downcast. The intervention of the complete stranger, who had attached himself to the dancer, had driven Zalman and his song-play out of everyone's thoughts. No one was paying the lad any heed.

The square, wood-beamed taproom was almost empty. In front of the large clay oven in the middle of the room several wagoners were stretched out, mouths open, beards disheveled. Flies ran over their coarse faces and buzzed round their legs and big noses, unintimidated by the rumbling of the wagoners' bellies and the snores issuing from their throats.

Nearby, two fattened geese padded about in a

* In Jewish folklore, Haman's son Dalfon was a synonym for pauper—the Hebrew word *dal* means "poor" —and Haman's tenth son, Vaisasa, was considered the personification of stupidity.

large, wooden cage, raising a cloud of dust whenever they spread and fluttered their wings. Oat husks, feathers, and down floated through the air.

In one corner of the taproom several personages were sitting over a pitcher of beer and a bowl of food. In a second corner a postillion, leaning on the handle of his sword, which was taller than himself, was watching two comrades throw dice.

Mine host, Michel the innkeeper, held a wooden bung between his teeth as he tapped wine from a big-bellied barrel into a container, whence it ran with a bubbling sound into a tin pitcher. With a movement of his eyes and the bung between his teeth, Michel gestured to his wife in dumb show, to serve the pitchers. She was sitting with uncovered breasts on an unmade tester-bed, suckling a baby. The infant attacked his mother's teat with his small mouth, delightedly kneading the breast with his fist. The inn-keeper's wife pulled herself away from the child, who began to cry bitterly.

Buxom and barefooted, the innkeeper's wife grasped the foaming pitchers and set out for the table where Fishel and his comrades were sitting. In her haste, she had neglected to button her dress, and the brown nipples of her breasts protruded from the white softness of her body like baked raisins.

"And what do you think of this ethrog tip?" Moshel nudged Fishel, laughing up his sleeve.

"Bite it off, you silly ass!" Fishel took a swig from the pitcher. He laid his hand on that of the lady of the house. "How does it happen, dear hostess," he inquired innocently, "that meat and dairy dishes are served together in a Jewish taproom?"

"Heaven forfend, sir!" she cried, opening a pair of large, innocent eyes.

"And what is this, pray?" Fishel pointed to the bare nipples oozing milk. "Isn't this meat with milk?"

Moshel bleated like a sheep. The Regensburg Maecenas doubled over; too far gone for laughter, his face was drenched with tears. Beside himself, he rumbled in a deep baritone:

"Oh, that's good! Oh, is that good!"

The dancer took Fishel first by one ear and then by the other, and rushed to the defense of her sex.

"Little Fishel, with his waggery! You vulgarian! You. . . . Just see how the poor creature is blushing!"

And indeed the mistress of the tavern was aflame with embarrassment. Though she found it difficult to button up, she was not at a loss for a reply:

"No one asked you to be a glutton!"

"Nor a pig, either!" the dancer chimed in.

"You needn't have flesh with milk, like a Gentile," the innkeeper's wife added, warming to the business of her reply.

"But what if a person has an overpowering urge for food, mistress mine?"

"Then there's roast hen, and there's goose." The mistress' dark eyes grew playful as she entered into the jest. "We'll never let you leave the Golden

Deer hungry. Well, masters, what will you have?"

"On the rich man's account," cried Fishel, pointing to Sachse, "a roast goose!"

Sachse, still wiping his tear-filled eyes, was busy chatting with the dancer. He had a foot in the door at the Elector's court, he informed her confidentially. Since he was purveyor of precious stones to the castle, there would be no difficulty at all in worming the dancer into court.

"What say you, Master Lemelin Sachse?" The mistress was impatient to go; her child had been crying ever since she left. "Shall I fetch a goose?"

"If the jesters wish goose, there's nothing more to say." Drinking down a beaker of wine, Lemelin sat back, ungirdled, and at his ease. "Now, Prague folk, don't you put Regensburg to shame! All week the wealthiest folk and rabbis from all Ashkenaz have been arriving for the wedding."

The odor of freshly roasted goose filled the taproom, and the crowd sniffed with pleasure. Fishel tapped out the Death Dance tune on the table with his fingers. In a low, very low voice, he pleaded with Rosa:

"I'm not frightened of this world, but of the hereafter.
For here my lot is hunger, need, and disaster.
O, shoot a wrathful arrow from your lovely bow,
And send me off to Paradise, as fast as I may go."

Rosa sank her teeth in the browned goose skin, and answered in an even lower voice:

"Paradise is full of such fools as thee.
Thou must stand without—there's no room for
*   thee.*
If thou'rt cold in this life, my fair,
Off to Hell with you—'twill be hot enough
*   there!"*

One of the two dice-players rose and left. The other stood up and pulled his loose cloak tightly about him, narrowing his shoulders. He pounded the table with both fists, sending the empty tankards leaping. Then he opened wide the mouth in his shaven, wrinkled face, and shouted words in the priestly Roman tongue like a battle cry:

"Meum est propositum in taberna mori."

"Rosa, a comrade!" Fishel stood up. "Let's invite him to join us at table."

Fishel slipped from behind the table and approached the Latinist. He bowed:

"In the name of the Nine Muses, O comrade. . . ."

"Who never desert us joculators, faithful servitors of the true words," replied the stranger.

"O comrade, honor and grace our table, sparkling with wine, odoriferous with roast goose."

"I never refuse a poet." The stranger took Fishel by the hand. "I shall gladly accompany thee, comrade."

The newcomer did not wait for a second invitation. Lifting the glass of wine that was handed him, he bowed to the dancer:

"To your health, lovely actor-girl, the only joy in this wanderer's life of ours. Your health—and the health of my little sister, Sabina, whom I have just removed from a nunnery and enrolled in a whorehouse. In the nunnery my sister became a whore, while remaining a holy woman. In the whorehouse, they will beat her and starve her— there, I trust, she will repent and mend her ways. Let's all drink to her health. My sister Sabina! Vivat, comrades!"

"Vivat! Vivat!" clinked the tankards and cups.

VI

Word spread through Jew Street immediately that rich Lemelin Sachse, that amateur bon vivant, was sitting in the Golden Deer taproom, munificently treating the Prague jesters to drinks and food. The news traveled from one frame house to its neighbor, reaching even the walls of Lemelin's own home.

In every street, wealthy, well-to-do, and ordinary common folk stood half-dressed at the open doors of their homes, showing various items of dress, presumably consulting about what to wear at the marriage ceremony. One woman held a silk dress, another a sleeveless velvet cloak, a third a pearl-embroidered collar. Actually, they were all amazed and quietly resentful at the patroness of

Regensburg, Master Samuel Belasser's wife, Gimchen. Here it was long past noon, and the wedding invitations had not yet been delivered by the invitation-bearer. Weren't her own townfolk good enough for her? Just because, as it was bruited abroad, pieces of cloth and tapestries had been imported from as far off as Stamboul for the wedding? Just because her husband, the Regensburg parness, had dealings with princes and kings? Was that the reason for this affront?

But not a word of this speculation passed their lips. Instead, they chatted about the Prague jesters; from this subject, they naturally passed to pretty Rosa, who had turned the heads of all the menfolk. In passing, the ladies demolished the reputation of half the town. Their mouths, eyes, fingertips, bodies flashed as they spun elaborate cobwebs of rumor and gossip with fierce delight—cobwebs so involved they could not extricate themselves.

"Here she comes!"

"The invitation-bearer is coming!"

The women recognized who it was from the tapping of her clog shoes. The invitation-bearer was a bent old woman, wearing an old-fashioned black cloak with a white ruffle around the neck. The ruffle was fastened to the cloak by a tin pin. Leaning on a crooked staff, the old woman opened her toothless mouth:

"Mistress Gimchen, our patroness, doth invite ye one and all to her daughter's espousal."

The old woman opened a kerchief, full of small coins, which she had been holding in her bony fist. As each woman threw in a coin or two, the invitation-bearer acknowledged the gift by opening and shutting her mouth like a fish, repeating time after time the formula:

> *"For this work of charity*
> *May you live to a hundred and twenty,*
> *With the help of God, keep your children in*
> *   plenty,*
> *And marry them off in prosperity."*

With a sigh of her whole sunken pious face, the old woman pointed her staff at Lemelin's door, where a wooden mezuzah in the shape of an ark hung on the doorpost.

"That such a lord and master as this may yet become parness of Regensburg—one that doth guzzle and swill with rogues and strolling actresses!"

"Our Lemelin?" inquired a neighbor.

"The very same Lemelin, 'tis a shame and disgrace." The old woman raised her voice in a loud Lamentations keening. "And the pretty actor-girl from Prague—may God strike her lame—doth amuse herself at Michel's inn."

"That apostate's gullet!" a woman cried out.

"Forgets all about his wife and children the moment he sniffs a thrashing young carp!" another interjected.

The neighbors huddled together, their feminine tongues wagging furiously. Ah, the pretty deeds Lemelin performs in Venice, where he busies himself purchasing amulets and precious stones for the Elector! And his wife, Rechlin—that puffed-up slut

—the airs she puts on! Not ashamed to brag that she is the apple of Lemelin's eye, that he keeps her in finery and jewelry, that he bedecks her with silver belts and gold stuff!

"Only Venice?" A well-fleshed Jewess with a mighty bosom pulled the knitted night cap down over her blond hair. "Lemelin consorts with girls, both Jewish and Gentile, in Regensburg, too! And when he has no other wine to bless, he makes do with a silly wench from Prague!"

"Is she a good-looking little woman, this Rosa-lein?" inquired a neighbor.

"Good-looking?" The invitation-bearer took offense on behalf of the female sex. "The actor-girl from Prague is a piece of baggage! She's a good-looking trundle-bed!"

At which all these pious-faced women, forever preaching morality, held their sides and breasts in vast amusement, their laughter pealing up to the sky. The well-fleshed Jewess pounded on the closed door of Lemelin's home, shrilling in a high-pitched voice quite out of keeping with her broad-limbed frame:

"Rechlin! Rechlin!"

A bolt creaked, and the door opened a crack, Rechlin put out her lovely face with its peaches and cream complexion. At the sight of the neighbors surrounding the invitation-bearer, her transparent, wine-colored eyes laughed sympathetically. The small double chin above her pearl-covered white neck trembled.

"Ha-ha-ha! What good tidings from the invitation-bearer?"

There was a moment of silence. The women wiped tears of laughter from their eyes with their fingers and aprons. Each waited for the other to begin. The old woman turned around, leaning on her staff, and resumed the Lamentations keening, as though she had not been interrupted.

"Dear children, you will do well to hearken— when a woman, be she actor-girl, or witch, or the very Queen of Sheba herself, steals a husband's love from his wife, there is a charm to employ—it is tested and proven. . . ."

"I should like to hear this," Rechlin whispered down to a neighbor, with a short laugh.

"Do tell us, Grandmother!"

"Make it worth my while, and I'll enjoy the telling." The old woman pointed to her money kerchief.

Rechlin felt for a coin in the deep, satin charity-pouch that hung from her waist on a silken thread. She gave the coin to the old woman, as to a fortune teller. The old woman spat three times. Then, her tongue moving up and down between her lips like a bell-clapper, she recounted her tale of magic:

"When the she-devil Lilith desires to break up a happy marriage, she dresses herself as an actor-girl, or as the Queen of Sheba, if necessary. Thus disguised, she can lead a very saint off the straight and narrow—much less a lively youth or an idler. The pious wife who finds herself in this unhappy state must take a mirror, and go off to the fields. There, when the sun is shining and butterflies dance and flutter about her, she must bury the mirror deep in the ground, like a corpse. And so doing, she must recite three times:

" 'With this mirror I bury the love that Mistress Venus bears for Tannhauser. And I pray Almighty God, blessed be His Holy Name, to restore peace to my home and my husband's heart.' "

"That very thing happened to Fulda," one of the women cried out.

"And in Worms, too, the town where I was born."

The old woman leaned more heavily on her crooked staff. "Listen to my tale:

"In a house near the well-spring, named Devil's Head, lived a pitiful pauper. Once upon a time this pauper went into his shop, which was in that house where he lived, and shed bitter tears of woe. As he was thus weeping over his dire poverty, who should appear but the Queen of Sheba herself. No lovelier woman had he ever seen in his life. Her hair was pure spun gold.

"She said: 'If you agree to sleep with me every noon when the clock strikes twelve, I will take you as husband, and make you rich beyond compare.'

"So the poor man allows himself to be seduced. Every noon when the clock strikes twelve, the Queen of Sheba appears. Two virgins follow her, carrying a golden basin filled with her gold and jewels. When she lies with the poor man, they place the basin on the ground near the bed. The virgins leave. The Queen of Sheba forbids the poor man to inform any living soul, on pain of death. Every day he does her will. And the Queen of Sheba keeps her word to the poor man. She brings him an abundance of gold and silver. He becomes rich and dresses both himself and his wife in a style befitting rich folk. His wife's hands sparkle with rings on Sabbaths and holy days.

"Once it came about that his wife asked the former pauper: 'Tell me, my dear husband, what is it you do in the shop every noon when the clock strikes twelve?'

"Replied the good man: 'I have grown accustomed to a noonday nap.'

"The wife asks no more about it. But she thinks to herself: 'There must be some reason why he goes to the shop the same time every day.' So, at the first opportunity, she slips the shop key from her husband, and has a locksmith fashion another just like it. Then, shortly after her husband has entered the shop, she follows, slowly opening the door with her own key. She enters, and beholds her husband lying with the Queen of Sheba. She also sees the gold basin with gold and jewels. Slowly the woman creeps out of the shop, slowly she closes the door behind her, so as not to wake them.

"Still and all, when the Queen of Sheba awakes, she says to the man: 'Now you must die. For you have revealed our secret. Someone has been here and has seen us sleeping together.'

"The man swears he is innocent, he knows nothing about it. He falls at her feet and the Queen of Sheba spares his life. But she declares: 'You shall never see me again, and all you wealth will disappear. You will become even poorer than you were before. I have borne you two children. I shall strangle them by the neck until they die. In three days, you must go to the bridge over the Rhine, and you will see a coffin drifting in the water. Therein will lie the children that I bore you. I shall bury them hard by the Rhine.'

"On the third day the man goes to the Rhine and sees the coffin floating on the water. And soon thereafter he turns into a woeful pauper again.

"And so, Jewish daughters, let none of you permit yourself to be seduced by money. The Lord, blessed be His Name, allots everyone the fortune proper to him."

The women had formed a ring around the invitation-bearer as she told her tale, listening with mouths and ears wide open in delight. Now, gulping down the old woman's words as gospel truth, each begged the good Lord to keep her husband from being seduced by a strolling woman.

"The things that happen!" one woman said with a sigh.

"At this moment, I wish I had my husband at my side," another remarked, and immediately became shame-faced.

"Is it true that Rosalein, the actor-girl from Prague . . ." Rechlin began. She stopped in the middle of her thought, twisting the rings on her fingers, reversing them.

"True, true," a neighbor cried out. "Rosalein sports with strange men."

"She's at Michel the innkeeper's now, drinking, singing, and dancing," added a second woman.

"And your Lemelin is there too," a third woman finished.

"My Lemelin?" The color fled from Rechlin's fair face. "I'm going straight there! And if I see them in the taproom together. . . ." She raised a monitory fist.

No one spoke. For a moment Rechlin regarded her neighbors, uncertain as to whether they might not be poking fun at her. She turned and swept into her home through the open door.

The heavy door banged shut. There was a screeching of the iron bolt. Rechlin's neighbors regarded one another apprehensively, as though sharing the common guilt of having trampled on a living creature. The old woman who had borne the invitations to Master Samuel Belasser's wedding ran two fingers along the wooden mezuzah on Lemelin's doorpost, and began to leave, her heavy clog shoes tapping as she shuffled off. Her sunken mouth mumbled:

"Good, good. Let the silly woman know about her saint Lemelin, too—can't bake cookies without fire. . . . You can bake nothing without fire, nothing at all."

VII

Michel of the Golden Deer ran his sticky hands over his sweating forehead and wet face, leaving marks behind. Then he wiped his fingers in his yellow beard; one corner of the beard, unkempt, stuck up.

He was standing in the cupolated alcove, pulling bungs out of barrels and tuns, tapping wine and beer into pouring vessels, thence into pitchers of tin and earthenware. When the liquor overflowed the pitchers, Michel dashed the foam off with a practiced thumb, and shouted the length of the room to his wife:

"Ready, Pessel, ready!"

In the happy confusion of business, Michel was so distraught he never noticed that one of his stockings had rolled down from his knee pants, uncovering a hairy shin.

It was a long time since business had thrived so. The leather pouch that hung on a strap over his shoulder was bulging, and could not be closed. And the take, the real money, was just beginning to roll in. Confused with the problems of making change, he ceased even to worry about his wife, who was chatting with strange men, drinking toasts in the company of the wealthy, pale-faced Sachse, and sporting with the jesters, despite their filthy, lewd speech.

In-laws from half of Bavaria, who had ridden into Regensburg for the parness' daughter's wedding, sat around tables large and small, enjoying the food and drink.

The jesters' small table was surrounded on every side by curious onlookers.

Rich Sachse had put a coral necklace around the dancer's neck; now, holding her hands tight, he was far gone in his cups. His thievish eyes glowed like live coals; his curly beard was pitch-black; red, fleshy lips protruded from his beard's darkness, in complete incongruity with his long, thin face, pale, drained of color.

First he told the dancer of his journeys, his great wealth—of Venice, of Mantua. Then he went on to tell of the Elector, ever on the lookout for dancers and musicians to lend fame to his Bavarian court. Personally, Lemelin Sachse was sure that Rosalein would please and captivate the Elector. She surpassed all the court girls in her ability to sing and dance. Access was all that was needed—and he, Lemelin, the Elector's purveyor. . . .

"But how could *I* ever be accepted in a royal court—just a common dancer without manners—and Jewish, besides?" Rosalein asked softly, raising her face to his.

Through the open window the rays of the sun shone ripe with the afternoon heat, bearing the smell and taste of honey. Sunbeams passed over Rosalein's lovely face, so lovely. . . . Her cheeks took on a pinkish tinge in the sunlight, like the skin of fresh, ripe peaches.

With a certain suspicion, Rosa accepted the attentions of this strange person—this dark-skinned, red-lipped giant who held her hands in his vise-like grip. It occurred to her that Fishel must be angry; he was drinking furiously, and gritting his teeth. But who knew? Rosalein had had a companion, a dancer like herself, who had gained entry into a prince's court, and had been elevated.

"Why so sad, Rosalein?" Little tongues of flame flickered in Lemelin's eyes. "Was not Anselmo del Pomis a jester, who recited and sang at feasts and weddings? And did *he* not gain entry to the Mantua court? Had it not been for the nobel lady Benvenida Abravanel, who introduced him at court, he would still be a jester today! I, Lemelin, the Elector's purveyor, will present you, my child. Do you hear, Rosalein? My lovely girl!"

All at once, the entire company of jesters appeared in the taproom. First came the stilt-walker, hopping on his long stork feet. He was followed by the flutist, the fiddler, the jew's harpist, the fire-swallower, the hydrocephalic dwarf. Last appeared the fortune teller, leading a monkey by the chain. He muttered:

"Pumay, you monkey, show what you've got
To make the decent folk laugh a lot."

"Fishel, who is treating?" inquired the stilt-walker, pointing to the scraps of the food on the table.

"Not me," grumbled Fishel.

The hungry jesters descended on the table like vultures. In the flash of an eye they had cleared off the scraps, gnawing the meat around the bones, cracking the bones and sucking the marrow. They were all thirsty for a glass of wine or a tankard of beer. The tin and clay pitchers on the table gleamed empty. Everywhere in the taproom, at side tables, well-fed rich folk sat, eating portions of carp or goose-quarters and washing them down with gallons of wine. Their stomachs were bursting.

"Well there, jesters," cried one of these well-satisfied in-laws, as he rose to loosen his waist girdle and jovially pushed his four-cornered hat down over his ears. "How about a song?"

"Let him who drinks sing," retorted a jester angrily.

"Here, now, you over-filled drinking companion . . ." the in-law extended a hand to the jester, "don't get so angry."

"Since I've had nought to drink, I'm no drinking companion," the jester replied, somewhat mollified.

"Right you are!" The in-law cordially came over to join the jesters. "One good deed deserves another. We have a song coming to us, and you have wine and dice coming to you."

"Fishel! Fish-el dear!" Rosa sang out coaxingly, eyeing Fishel so tenderly he squirmed in his seat.

"Fish-el dear!" The dwarf in short silk trousers stood up on the table and grimaced in imitation of the dancer. "Fishel, Fish-el dear, don't be so proud, I've been Jewished too!"

The crowd roared with laughter:

"Good for him! Bravo!"

Fishel turned over an empty pitcher, mouth down, and clapped on the empty tin for them all to be quiet. His melancholy eyes swept from face to face, finally coming to rest on the well-fed in-law, who had been talking all the while.

"Master in-law, instead of talking so much, treat the jesters to wine and beer!"

When it grew quiet, Fishel hugged the empty pitcher to his breast. His clear, deep voice filled the taproom:

"Good wine, old wine, strong wine,
Has been subdued by water.
No song can fill this mouth of mine—
'Tis full of water, water!"

The company of jesters opened their dry mouths and the taproom echoed to the refrain:

"I have no wine—these eyes of mine,
I have no wine—these eyes of mine
Are full of water, water!"

The crowd paused, mouths open, waiting for Fishel to continue; but he stood mute, trying to catch Rosa's eye. When she finally raised her eyes to his, he shrugged, swept the empty pitchers toward him, and sang to them:

"I cannot swallow my food dry;
Bread has not taste with water.
I raise the beaker to the sky—
Filled with water, water."

Now the whole taproom joined in the chorus, tapping the beat with pitchers and legs:

"I have no wine—these eyes of mine
Are full of water, water.
I have no wine—these eyes of mine. . . ."

"No water! Wine, the best wine in the house!"
The ungirdled in-law called to the innkeeper's wife.

She was standing flushed, mouth agape.
Though the singing had stopped, she continued to
wave the empty pitchers she held in both hands to
the rhythm. Her eyes were fixed on Lemelin, who
held the dancer tight as he continued to whisper
promises in her ear. In her abstraction, the innkeeper's wife did not hear the cry for wine.

The in-law jovially embraced the innkeeper's
wife, and pulled her to him:

"Wine, mistress! The crowd is thirsty for some
wine!"

Abashed, the good wife squirmed in his arms.
Lifting the empty pitchers, she defended herself
from his advances, a blush spreading over her face.
But he would not let her go, and bending over her
body, tried to kiss her; ludicrously his own beard
got in the way of his eyes and mouth.

The crowd stamped their feet, clapped hands,
and whistled:

"Listen to him panting!"

"Ha-ha-ha—what's that he smells?"

"The goodwife is no lily of the valley!"

The crowd waited with delight for the innkeeper to come running up. But at that moment,
Rechlin, rich Lemelin's wife, swept into the taproom. It was some time before she caught sight of
her husband, in close company with the dancer. The
words sprang from her tight lips:

"His hour is up!"

Little Rechlin assailed the couple with such

impetus that Rosalein had no time to rise, much less to defend herself. Clutching fingers tore at her hair as she sat paralyzed. The words flamed before her eyes:

"Brazen creature! Fond of strange men, are you, hussy? Adulteress!"

Lemelin sobered up on the spot. He moved back, trying to put as much distance as possible between himself and his wife. Fishel appeared on the scene, yelling to his comrades.

"Ignoramuses! Idiots!" He cried in priestly Latin. Then he passed to their Yiddish mother tongue. "Oxen! Cattle! Why do you let them fight? Do you want our Rosa to be murdered!"

But before the knot of jesters could gather just what was happening, the dancer was standing with hair disheveled, disdainfully watching the little woman stride to the door, her lanky, overgrown husband shuffling after her.

"But what's this?" Fishel lifted Rosa's arm, which was dripping blood.

" 'Tis nought, Fishel, nought." Rosa looked at the dark red drops, her eyes smiling. "This is my payment for a string of beads. In this world of ours, you get nought for nought. . . . Nought."

Fishel took Rosa into the forehouse. There at the faucet he washed her scratched arm, feeling as he did so that his own skin was bleeding.

Impetuously, Rosa suddenly embraced Fishel; the peaked cap fell off his head. She kissed him on the eyes, the mouth, the beard. Before he could recover, she was gone, leaving only her breath behind, the whisper:

"Fishel, Fishel, my dear Fishel."

VIII

Jew Street, leading to Master Belassar's courtyard, was impassible. The iron gate stood wide open. On either side of the gate were stationed two knights wearing short coats, creased pants, and bell-shaped hats, all of red velvet. Swords hung over the coats. These knights, Belasser's servants in costume, held back the uninvited crowd that pushed and shoved in an attempt to enter the courtyard.

The house, constructed of square, rough-hewn stones, with a tower at each corner, stood deep in the courtyard. Overgrown with moss, its crumbling walls gave the building the appearance of a deserted old castle.

The crowd had been gathering since early morning. Like vultures, poor folk attacked the watchroom and dance house. The townsfolk, jostling one another, gathered in front of the iron gates. Everywhere men, women, and children stood about, watching and waiting.

So magnificent a procession, so rich a display of precious stones and wealth had never before been seen in Regensburg. There were in-laws from Worms, from Frankfort-on-the-Main, from distant Vienna, and even from far-off Stamboul.

Wherever you turned your eyes, you saw velvet and silk. Everywhere you looked, you caught sight of gold- and silver-embroidered cloaks, wide Spanish sashes in black, white, and scarlet. Doors were continually opening and shutting. The womenfolk, particularly, came and went—young girls, matrons, grandmothers, with diamond earrings that fell over their spangled shoulders, with tight-fitting sleeves circled at the elbow by gold bracelets set with emeralds and rubies. Neck after neck was adorned by pearls, or amber beads with dangling golden guilder coins.

"Pessalin!" A girl embraced her friend. "What is it, darling? Why so sad?"

"I, sad?" Pessalin raised a pair of melancholy, dark eyes. "Do you think it's envy because I have no money, no diamonds, no silk, no satin? Or that all my clothes are old rags?" She ran her hand over her knee. "That doesn't trouble *me!* But Yentele, I have such a longing for beads—red, bright red corals, like the kind Master Hanover's daughter Faygelin is wearing."

"Corals?" Yentele's red lips were a thin line of deprecation. "I have no worries about corals! No joking, Pessalin! If I merely said the word, Belasser's servant would give them to me!"

"Who—that fine fellow Zalman?" Pessalin pointed to one of the "knights" guarding the gate. "You ought to scratch the servant's eyes out!"

"The rascal would dearly love to pass the time with me," Yentele laughed decorously. "But— nought, nought! She who wishes to break a maidenhead may do so with him—that worn-out capon! But not I—not Yentele!"

The head of the yeshiva arrived, dressed in a black cloak. He was leading a young man covered in a white silken garment that reached down to his ankles. The young man's wide sash was white, the turban on his head vermillion red. His eyes, beard, and earlocks—all were pitch black.

Suddenly it grew still on Jew Street, as the observers held their collective breath, and pricked up their eyes and ears. The silence was broken by the howling of an infant.

"What's the screaming about? Sounds like a woman in labor!" Complaints poured in on the terrified mother from every side. "Either give the babe to suck, or off with you!"

"Hush, hush," someone called out. "The poor thing has the whooping cough."

"Then take him to a doctor!" came the advice. "Cupping will do him no harm!"

In anxious desperation, a short, thin woman thrust a dry breast into the infant's mouth. Her small black mouse eyes stared in confusion at the stranger accompanying the head of the yeshiva.

Everyone's glance was directed at the fascinating stranger.

"Who may he be?"

"Master Yekel," the crowd stopped the old sexton, and pointed at the stranger. "Who may he be, Master Yekel?"

"He? Why, that is Rabbi Kalman! Our own Rabbi Kalman of Regensburg."

"That is he?"

"The cabalist? Who lives in Stamboul now?"

"Why, he is still very young!"

"What noble features!"

"And he comes of good lineage!"

"And wealth!"

"Wealth?" Master Petachiah, a famous pauper who had been to the Holy Land twice, burst into laughter. "This Rabbi Kalman would have been re- nowned for wealth in the very court of King Ar- thur!"

A small circle formed around Master Peta- chiah, and a still larger circle around the first. Someone inquired:

"Is it true, Master Petachiah, that Rabbi Kal- man is carrying a writ from the King of Turkey to the Jews throughout Ashkenaz?"

"It's true, it's true!"

"A lover of Israel, the Turk!"

"Why not?" Disheveled, his clothes in disar- ray, Master Petachiah raised his hairy hands in en- thusiasm. His dark eyes glowed. "These are the days of the Messiah, come at last. The simple man who wishes a bit of land of his own, or to traffic in com- merce undisturbed, or to reside a stone's throw from the Holy Land, need but let our sweet Ash- kenaz rot where it is and remove to Constantino- ple."

"What do we have here, anyway?"

"Here?" Everything about Petachiah fell to laughing—his careworn face, the very patches of beard on his cheek. "Here? Here we have poll tax and protection tax. If a Jew makes a profit, he must give every third pfennig to the German sot. Go to the Square on business, and you aren't sure of your life. Everywhere, scoundrels, rascals, dunces, tricksters, villains! And at nightfall, when the ghetto gates are locked, the women strain their eyes with longing to see their husbands return in peace. It's a shame and a disgrace! And they say," Master Petachiah whispered the rumor, "all the Jews in Regensburg, over five hundred households, are to be deported!"

"God be with us!" sighed a Jewess.

At the word "deported," they forgot that Regensburg was wedding with Worms that day, that in-laws had come hither from all of Ashkenaz, that the Prague jesters had arrived. Weeping and shouting echoed in their ears—not that of Regensburg alone, or the town of Speyer, but the suffering of cities and towns from which Jews had been driven out in the recent past. In their imagination, they saw terrified and helpless eyes, the eyes of those wakened by a fire in the middle of the night. . . . But the trepidation of the people of Regensburg was short-lived, Happiness at the wedding, joy for the bridal couple —perhaps it was the festive occasion, but whatever the reason, they immediately discovered a bright side in the threatened catastrophe. Well, what if they should be driven out of Regensburg? There was a Creator in Heaven, and he had already opened wide the gates of Constantinople for them, crying, "Come, come, dear children, and see how I have elevated the Jew! Muhammed the Second has

made place for all three faiths next to his throne—
the mufti, the rabbi to the right, the Greek Orthodox patriarch to the left."

Next to arrive was a man in a loose black-and-
white striped garment, resembling a tallith, whose
collar came down over the shoulders, and whose
sleeves ballooned out. He wore a sable hat at an
angle. Pouches of herbs and bags of amulets hung
from his black sash. Plying his elbows and staff, this
individual pushed through the crowd. He wiped his
black, wide, long beard, and licked his thick lips.
The striped, loose sleeves of his gown flew through
the air, and his thin white hands fluttered accompaniment to a deluge of words that had a foreign
ring to the Ashkenazic ear. "Finds, pious ladies,
finds—I have finds for you!"

"This must be the healer!"

"No, 'tis the Ripper—the doctor!"

"The Pole?"

The words came rushing forth, in a long
string:

"Amulets handwritten in Safed, handwritten in
Jerusalem. Tried and tested herbs from the grave of
Rabbi Simeon ben Yochai. Good for gall stones,
jaundice, constipation. Black deer-horn cramp
thimbles, guaranteed to drive pain from aching
loins and joints. Meteorites. . . ." The healer's voice
turned soft and deep. "All colors: sky-blue, rainbow, blood-red. A charm to ease childbirth—no
Jewish daughter need abort, heaven forfend! Red
shooting stars are seen falling no more. When the
Holy Temple in Jerusalem stood in flames, the

blessed Lord sent down a hail of shooting stars. That, O pious women, is where the redness comes from—the flames. Should it go hard with a woman in labor, just lay the meteor stone on her naked body, and the stone shoots sparks, and it's 'Welcome and farewell' to the demon Lilith and her daughters. Come pious women, come running and buy, while they last—I have finds, finds, finds!"

As the young women gathered around the doctor, he bent over to a young woman who was far gone in pregnancy and, in stage whisper that set everyone smiling, said:

"And if a young wife has a husband with a roving eye, here's a red shooting star to win his heart back again."

Meanwhile, some women brought the sick child to the healer for him to examine. Regarding the child's crooked little legs and swollen belly, he asked the mother:

"What's wrong with the child?"

"He has the whooping cough."

"Whooping cough?" The doctor quickly drew a flask of schnaps, a glass, and a lancet from his sash. He extended a hand toward the sympathetic women. The coins fell into his palm as he declared reassuringly:

"Lancing is a complete cure for whooping cough. A complete cure! There's nought bad in it at all!"

The doctor scratched the lobe of the child's left ear with his lancet. A drop of blood oozed out. The doctor placed the drop in the glass of schnaps and

stirred with a finger. With his wet finger he wiped
the child's lips. Then the doctor rubbed the potion
over the child's swollen body; but the child
screamed so, jerking and squirming with pain, that
the mother gathered him in her arms and fled home.

The words flew through the air:

"The jesters! The Prague jesters are coming!"

Small fry emerged from every nook and
cranny. Spinning like tops, they broke into song:

"Flute
Trumpet,
Actor-girl—
Here they come!
Here come the jesters from Prague!"

The jesters played jokes on the small fry. The
stilt-walker strode over the children's heads, shoo-
ing them away:

"Off to the schoolroom, mousies! Off to the
schoolroom with you!"

Leering at the crowd, the dwarf sang:

"My lords and masters, such things I'll show to
ye,
As will make young and old laugh with glee!"

The folk from Prague passed through the gate.
Close on their heels a company of beggars pressed
to enter the courtyard. They battled the two liveried
servitors, who drove off the beggars with the taunt:

"Off to the dance hall with you, counts and
ragbags! To the dance hall! You'll be served hens
and fish at a covered table!"

"Hens and fish!" A yellow beggar, whose dress showed him to be a Pole, grimaced at one of the servitors, and flung an empty sleeve in his face. "Tells us guests where to go, does he? Conniptions take him!"

"A cramp in your innards!" cried a second beggar.

"Worms eat you!" added a third.

The servitor spurred his white horse, which reared on its hind legs and struck its forelegs out at the beggars. They retreated to the servitor's angry shout:

"Off with you, tatterdemalions! Off with you, dogs! No cursing here! No ranting! No foaming at the mouth!"

The yellow beggar fled with the rabble to the other side of the street, his empty sleeve waving in the wind. Irrepressible, he opened a gap-toothed mouth and mimicked:

"No ranting! No foaming at the mouth! Dogs, are we? We'll shit on your grave! And on your master's grave, too!"

The folk from Prague swept through long, arched corridors, climbed dark, dizzying stairs, and opened door after door until they entered the Belasser apartment. The rooms were wide and bright, some long enough for a four-wheeled, spanned wagon to turn a complete circle. Yet from the street, the building looked so narrow that the observer would have deemed such expansiveness and spaciousness unimaginable.

In one hall the menfolk were gathered, in another the women and girls. The Prague jesters practised on their instruments in an alcove near the women's hall; rehearsing their skits, they prepared to surpass their local Regensburg fellows. The Regensburg "forces," for their part, gathered in the alcove near the men's hall. There, Master Leib and his troupe rehearsed pieces from the "Samuel Book," in loud, singsong tones.

The last bright rays of sunlight shone through the open, narrow windows. The people, the tapestries, the dramatic gestures—all glowed in the gentle warmth of the setting sun. Heavy silver candelabra standing on corner tables were already lit; their silver branches reflected the small candle flames, faint in the sunlight.

Moshel Cracower moved busily from room to room, beside himself with the importance of the task of bringing Leib and Fishel together. Both performers were reluctant. Master Leib refused to dignify the Prague players with any term other than "that band of jesters," or "those rogues from Prague."

Fishel, for his part, made a great show of having forgotten Leib's name—he referred to him as "that braggart who writes chit-chat for old women." Still, at bottom, Fishel was eager to be introduced to Leib.

When Moshel took his former schoolmate by the shoulder, Fishel pretended ignorance as to where Moshel was taking him. As they approached the other alcove, Moshel called out:

"Master Leib!"

Leib, with the impressive mien of the head of a yeshiva, came into the hall. The pleated black coat that reached down to his knees was fastened at the neck by a bone button the size of a reichsthaler coin. His white face with the transparent skin was framed in a silken black beard in which every hair fluttered at the slightest breeze.

"May I introduce Fishel Singer of the folk from Prague," said Moshel hurriedly, terrified lest the two come to words on the spot.

"I've heard of him, I've heard of him." Leib negligently put out his fingertips to Fishel. "What have you brought with you, Praguer? Any fresh bake-meats?"

"No bake-meats at all," little Fishel drew himself up to his full height, on a level with Leib. "No bake-meats, Master Leib. We bear old wine—good old Hildebrandt, good old Dietrich."

"Hildebrandt, Dietrich—old wine?" Leib grimaced. "They're old hens, that yield neither eggs nor flesh!"

Fishel's color changed. He lost his tongue in the presence of the comrades who had gathered round. Here stood Rosalein and the stilt-walker, and Zalman, the red-headed boy who had written *Amnon and Tamar*. What right had Leib to stick his nose up in the air? What if he *was* a head taller than Fishel? Fishel could always be Leib's match. He clenched his teeth, to hold back the biting, harsh words on the tip of his tongue. And the longer Leib talked about King David, and Judah Maccabeus,

and Bar Kochba, the less inclined Fishel was to
loosen his sharp tongue. Seduced by Leib's words,
Fishel listened open-eared.

In essence, all Leib really wanted was for
Fishel to concede that the old Jewish heroes, men
like King David and Judah Maccabeus, were war-
riors as valiant as any German kings or princes.
And what about Bathsheba? Did not the lovely
Krimhilde, and the still lovelier Brunehilde, pale in
comparison with our Bathsheba? In the words of
King David, as reported in Master Leib's own
"Samuel Book": "Bathsheba—I have seen no love-
lier personage than thee in all my days!"

"But Fishel swears that *I* am the loveliest!"
Rosalein's eyes sparked.

"You *are* the loveliest," cried the dwarf in-
stantly, and the company burst into laughter.

Fishel did not reply. His customary bravado
had left him, and he felt himself in truth shorter
than Leib, like an apprentice in the presence of his
master. Leib, refusing to be interrupted, and sens-
ing all the comrades on his side, ended his speech
with an indignant outcry:

"Since that is so, comrades, and we all agree
that we have such wealth in our own midst, what
need have we to make a Hildebrandt and a Dietrich
into Jews—we have our own David, our own Judah
Maccabeus, our own Bar Kochba!"

"Right!"

"Master Leib is right!"

"Vivat Master Leib!" And Rosalein embraced
the new hero.

Berl the sexton called out:

"Make way for Yosilman Roseheim, our parness and leader!"

The men's hall filled with excitement at the unexpected announcement. The rabbis, the head of the yeshiva, the in-laws from Stamboul, the bridegroom and attendants, the respected in-laws and affluent citizens—all rose, one by one. Young girls, dressed in colored silk dresses, rushed out of the other hall, like birds in full plumage. Belasser, in his capacity as the main in-law, lifted a burning candelabrum from the table and set out for the entrance to greet this most important guest. His wife, Gimchen, took his side, dressed in a costume of white silk and still whiter satin, whose folds and pleats rustled as she moved; sparkling, her deep, black eyes brought distant lands to mind. On her neck, white as milk, hung strands of pearls—pearls small as poppy seeds, pearls like tear drops, pearls like grapes, upon which blue-white flames shone with the colors of the rainbow. Husband and wife regarded each other with satisfaction. Belasser's eyes, his thin, grayish beard—everything about him shone. He had not expected so exalted a guest. Lifting the candelabrum higher, Belasser thanked the Lord for having granted him the great honor of having in his own house Master Yosilman Roseheim, the Jewish leader and parness, one who stood before kings, before emperors.

Yosilman's body servant, a huge individual, was about to remove the loose traveling cloak from his master's shoulders. But Yosilman retained his cloak, on which the yellow wheel—the Jewish sign—was conspicuously absent. The fringe of curls around his cheeks lent importance to the youthful face, whose gray eyes, with their expression of tenacity and endurance, expressed lofty amazement:

"Why all this honor for me?"

When the servant had removed the candelabrum, Yosilman let it be known that he was in haste, that he had not time, that he could remain in Regensburg only for an hour, or at the most an hour and a half—for he was traveling with the young Elector to Bavaria. He, Yosilman, had barely been able to persuade the Elector to make the stop in Regensburg; the espousal was but a pretext. There was serious talk of a deportation from Regensburg. Sinister powers were at work: the Princess Kunigunde, priests, converts, as well as run-of-the-mill anti-Semites. So Regensburg required an ally. And Elector Karl might well become king tomorrow or the day after. Therefore, let Belasser see to it immediately that a table fit for a king was set: the best exotic wines, the rarest fruits. And, most important, have the players perform a Death Dance. The Elector dearly loved the Jewish Death Dance.

A tumult arose. Forgotten were groom and bride, who stood forlorn among the agitated crowd —she, black of hair and black of eye, in white satin; he, blue of eye and light of hair, in black velvet. Slender, very slender—a blossoming twig—she leaned toward the groom, whispered in his ear, and gave him a small bag of salt, a charm to avert the evil powers. His smooth cheeks reddened, like a child's.

Light flowed from the oil lamps and candelabra, and was reflected on the walls, which were covered with leather embossed with dark-red floral patterns. Above the leather were long, narrow tapestries which pictured Moses bending barefoot before the burning bush, and Ruth falling at Boaz's feet.

No one noticed when Berl the sexton carried in the bridal canopy, nor when he fetched the communal shears to cut the sealed pouches wherein lay the dowry from the groom's side and the dowry from the bride's side. No one wondered why the rabbi was not writing the marriage contract.

All eyes were turned to the entrance, where a young knight, supple as a snake, swept into the room. His blinding, silver-scaled armor sparkled, his sword clattered. He was followed by a second knight, then by a third, and a fourth. The bodyguard stood at attention for the Elector, a very tall young man, with the long face of a thoroughbred. After the Elector came the officials of Regensburg, and after them the Jewish worthies: Yosilman the shtadlan, then Master and Mistress Belasser, then bride and groom, rabbis, and the in-laws from Stamboul.

Lemelin Sachse, who was often abroad on business and had knowledge of the ways of the world, was the first to remove his hat. All but the rabbis stood bare-headed as the knightly hall resounded to the cries of vivat:

"Hoch! High!"

At the head of the room stood the Elector, flanked by his bodyguard. Their swords glinted overhead, forming an arch. Under the lifted swords bride and groom walked, to the click of spurred boots, to bow before the Elector:

"Hoch! Hoch!"

Swords, candelabra, silverware, glassware, all shimmered. Mouths gaped, hands pressed together, eyes shone. Wine overflowed silver beakers, overflowed polished glasses, raised to toast the bride and groom. To the music of the flute, Fishel sang:

*"I open my lips to sing my sweet lay
In honor of groom and bride today.
Ho-hoch! Ho-hoch!"*

The bars between the men's hall and the women's hall were down. Knights and lords, lads and lasses, all moved easily from table to table, drinking, eating, joking, and laughing, in jubilation, in forgetfulness.

Almost unobserved, the sexton set up the bridal canopy and wrapped the narrow-necked "good-luck" glass in a piece of white linen. Almost unheard was his cry:

"In-laws on the bride's side, in-laws on the groom's side—now you may count the dowry in the best of spirits!"

The in-laws from Regensburg and Worms regarded one another dumbly, and concurred that there was no need to count their respective dowries at this time and place—they agreed to trust one another.

Braided waxen candles flickered.

"To the canopy! To the canopy!"

First came the music—fiddle, flute, jew's harp. Then the two fathers-in-law leading the groom. Then the two mothers-in-law with the veiled bride. Bringing up the rear, the drum with a skip and a beat. The fiddle wept, the flute wept, the jew's harp wept—all to drive off the evil spirits, the devils and demons that come from the north.

Knights drew swords from scabbards with a clanking. One cabalist rejoiced, quoting: *"Makshin befarzela*—there is beating on iron." Another cabalist rejoiced with another quote: *"Lehagen min hashedim makifin bebarzel*—to defend against demons one should beat on iron." The rabbi rocked to and fro as he recited the benediction—the spun-gold sacramental ring sparkled and trembled in the light. Wine flowed. A cabalist rejoiced, quoting again: *"Mamshichin yayin, lifne chasan vekalah*—one should pour wine before a bride and groom." The groom bent his pale face to the north, shattered the narrow-necked glass on the wall—Mazel Tov! Mazel Tov! Burnt wheat fell in a hail on their heads and faces. Now the fiddle laughed, the flute laughed, the jew's harp laughed:

Mazel Tov! Mazel Tov!

The tables and floor rugs were removed. The knightly hall became twice as long, twice as wide. Near the red-leathered walls sat the guests. Forgotten was the wedding, the canopy ceremony. Master and Mistress Belasser and the Regensburg dignitaries were impressed instead by the Elector's attentiveness to Yosilman, whom he pressed for the significance of each Jewish practice.

Lemelin Sachse captured the main in-law in a corner. He thrust a small gold watch set with diamonds into Belasser's hand:

"Only one thousand reichsthaler."

"That's too high, you ask too much." Belasser examined the watch.

"Too much?" Sachse's thievish eyes turned naïve. "This is a gift the Elector will never forget so long as he lives. Princes don't forget such things."

Belasser hesitated—should he or should he not make the Elector a present of the watch? Rapidly he said:

"In faith, I should be happy to do business with you. Would eight hundred reichsthaler be enough?"

Belasser's offer represented two hundred reichsthaler profit. Lemelin was delighted with the offer, but the merchant in him impelled him to say:

"Eight hundred? Offer one more hundred, Master Samuel, just one more hundred. I should like to get back my investment."

Belasser took the watch. Overwhelmed with delight, Lemelin ran busily to and fro—first to whisper in the Elector's ear, then to Belasser, then to the actor-girl, whom he hastened to assure that she was bound to please, the Elector would certainly take her into the royal court.

The folk from Prague were not at all happy with this turn of affairs. And Fishel, who was preparing to play the parts of the parness, jester, convert, and prophet in the Death Dance—Fishel, rummaging through the costumes, avoided Rosa. It did not matter to him at that moment that the local talent had been passed over and he, Fishel, not Leib, was to perform out front. He would happily have conceded everything—money, honor, applause—for one word from Rosa, one look, telling him that she would remain with him. He would gladly have left the wedding feast and the Elector, to go with Rosa, away from Regensburg.

He threw a side glance at Rosa, who was preening herself. She piled her black braids high, then tried coiling them around her lovely, small head. After ruffling through a half-dozen dresses, she stood before him in velvet, crying: "Fishel boy, which should I appear in, the velvet or the silk?" It was not every day that Rosa had such an opportunity. She was anxious to please the Elector and the "mighty" knights. Fishel ought not look at her with eyes so sad, as though the world were coming to an end. What if she did perform in the royal court? She would never forget him. And now, before they did the Death Dance, she was to present herself before the Elector and the counts. What did Fishel think? Why was he silent?

The fiddle burst into song. Then the flute. Then the jew's harp. Rosa ran into the hall like a gust of wind; suddenly, she stopped, and stood on tiptoe in front of the Elector. Her small, dark head was thrown back; her heart fluttered under the tight bodice of the velvet dress which fell from her shapely hips in airy folds to her ankles. Her body, swaying restless and seductive, took away the breath of the audience.

Alone, Rosa danced the Jew Dance. There was no leaping now, no slapping hands on thighs, no snapping of index finger against thumb. There was no place for these distractions in the Jew Dance as performed in Ashkenaz. Rosa swept over the red floor and swayed, one step to the right, one step to the left. Every turn of her body, every bend, conveyed both joy and sadness. Her eyes were alight; from deep in her throat she sang softly:

> *"High and noble Elector, would not ye*
> *Desire to come dancing with me?"*

The young Elector reddened. Before he could reply, Rosa had gone on to the knights:

> *"My gracious knights, would not ye*
> *Desire to come dancing with me?"*

Sword and harness clattered. The knights—an armored wall—were ready for the dance. Rosa advanced a step, retreated, elusive—catch me, catch me, if you can!—and disappeared in the alcove.

The hall shook to the shouting:

"Rosalein! Vivat Rosalein!"

"Vivat!"

Behind the shouting and turmoil threaded a still, distant weeping. It was the jew's harp, mourning in a side room, setting the mood for the Death Dance. The atmosphere grew uncanny. Eyes turned to the closed alcove, where Fishel, in the costume of a parness, sat in a corner drinking wine from a flask. He knew that after the Death Dance, Rosa would be leaving him. She had been raised up, had obtained entry into the royal court.

And he, Fishel? The royal court meant nothing to him. What to him was Elector, what were knights to him, when a profound melancholy seethed and burned within him? Rosa was leaving him, and he was suffering. The same wine that deadened his sadness awakened dormant powers; these, seizing him like a storm wind, broke through every barrier.

Fishel drank, and waited for a miracle. Rosa came and pleaded with him. The stilt-walker and drummer added their pleas for him to stop drinking: another gulp and Fishel would collapse—and all the Prague jesters would be humiliated. Well then, since they were pleading, he would insist that Rosa—Rosa do what? What *could* he demand? The words stuck in his throat. Rosa took him by one hand, then by the other.

"Fishel, Fish-el boy, my parness, my jester, my prophet! Come, they are waiting for us. Don't you hear the Death Dance tune?

He rose, tottering, and stood thus for a few moments. Then, against his will, the corners of Fishel's mouth turned up in a smile. A low, melancholy song trickled from behind his crooked white teeth:

"I cannot dance, I cannot jest,
Your sun is rising in the East,
Away, faithless Rosa. Away from me!
I'll have nought to do with such as thee!"

Rosa embraced Fishel. Facing him, breast to breast, she laughed in his face:

"Wilt have nought to do with such as me?
Thou goat!
Thou art no prophet, art a rutting stoat!
Thou shalt get many a pretty maid
To lie with thee, nor be gainsaid.
So dance with me, my whiskered goat...."

She pulled Fishel to the door. Wordlessly, he followed her. A shiver ran down her body at the look in his eyes.

The alcove door opened.

Rosa stood on the threshold, in a white silken shroud. The jew's harp wept Death's song of lamentation. Slowly, Rosa raised her arms out of the loose shroud—they were wings, tapering wings. She flew through the hall, a bat. In the smooth, impassive face the eyes, black, smoldering, darted here and there.

The Parness appeared. Death, with one wing high and one low, pursued the Parness. A chill wind ran through the hall. Was it Fishel she was pursuing? Rosa was uncertain. The Parness' beard was pitch-black, his sensual lips red, his stature immense —the Parness was a black ogre. No, this was not Fishel. This was Lemelin, Lemelin Sachse.

The Elector looked at Sachse, then at the

jester, and burst into laughter. The whole hall
laughed with him, as Lemelin, more concerned for
the jewels in his stuffed pockets than for his own
life, twisted and turned with trembling limbs, artfully avoiding the clutches of Death. The evil eyes
flamed, shot sparks—the fire of his eyes threatened
to singe Death's wings.

"Bravo!" shouted a knight.

"Bravo, vagrant! Bravo, strolling player!"

With outspread wings, Death thrust the Parness into a corner. He ran frantically back and
forth, as in a cage, trying to escape. Angrily he
cried:

> *"Now is no time for me to dance!*
> *I am not ready now to dance!*
> *There's business waiting me outside.*
> *The prince requires his body-tithe.*
> *The people call. I must obey.*
> *Let me be—I must away!"*

But Death, lifting one wing, then another, in
preparation for the dance, took the Parness by the
arm and sang:

> *"Come, Parness, come and dance with me.*
> *We'll twist and turn, so merrily.*
> *Twisting is your specialty.*
> *The people you have tended well*
> *Your pockets lined. And so farewell—*
> *Now let us dance, we two.*
> *And so farewell, and say farewell,*
> *All, rich or poor, must dance farewell*
> *With me. And so must you."*

Death led the Parness in a circle dance, brushing the floor in front of him with her wings. In the background, the jew's harp and fiddle, strummed by invisible musicians, played accompaniment. The strings trembled to the rapid movement of unseen fingers. The highest note drew its last breath, and the music expired. Death moved alone now, one wing up, one down, weaving its song of mourning. Death bowed before the Elector:

> "O, great Elector, mighty peer,
> Your strength is known to all.
> Come with me, and have no fear.
> I am the end of all.
> Yet serf of the Almightiest, whom no one may gainsay.
> When He commands, my mighty lord, great princes must obey."

The Elector rose, and after him Yosilman and the bodyguard. The hall resounded with applause and clapping. Swords flashed, spurs clicked:

"Bravo, Rosalein!"

"Bravo, actor-woman!"

"Bravo!"

Fishel, though he could scarcely keep his feet, was sobered by the applause. He retreated deep into the alcove, searching for an exit from Belasser's home. As he opened a side door, tall Leib came toward him.

"Whither, Fishel? Whither?"

Fishel did not reply.

They looked at one another as they listened to the walls resounding, the windows trembling, with the cries. Sadly they smiled in mutual understanding: this was but froth, ephemeral froth that comes and goes. Life, they knew, is no spendthrift. What it gives to one, it withholds from another. But eternity was theirs—Leib's and Fishel's.

Leib laid a hand on Fishel's shoulder:

"Stay with me, Fishel."

"Where? Here in Regensburg? In Ashkenaz?"

Leib walked a few steps with Fishel. At the stairs he stopped and talked freely of his plans. He did not intend to remain in Regensburg. For Leib, Ashkenaz meant far more than merely the cities on either side of the Rhine. To him, Ashkenaz was Italy, France, even Stamboul—wherever Yiddish was spoken. Leib had composed a "Samuel Book," and a "Bar Kochba Play," and was about to finish a play entitled, *Exile from Spain*. As Fishel could see, Leib was not setting forth empty-handed. Should there be need of a play-woman—Venice, Mantua, Rome could supply one. What was Rosalein compared with an Italian play-woman?

At the sound of Rosalein's name, Fishel's narrow body shuddered, his face contorted. Leib did not notice. He talked on. He would take Fishel, on one condition. There must be no poor rendering into Yiddish of Italian or German tales. If Fishel consented, they could take to the road tomorrow or the day after.

Fishel did not reply. The enthusiastic applause

within would not let him rest. He began going down the steps, Leib after him. When they left the court-yard, pushing with difficulty through the crowd, Fishel suddenly turned to Leib:

"We leave, we leave—the sooner the better!"

Ciechanow Melody

It was late Friday when Wolf Landau awoke, stretched, and lay in bed with his disheveled head thrown back.

Friday was his day of rest. The orthodox Jewish newspaper on whose editorial staff he worked was closed. That day he generally enjoyed the luxury of having breakfast in bed, reading poetry, and lazing about until afternoon. But this Friday he could not enjoy his day off. He had an oppressive obligation to meet.

Or perhaps it was not really an obligation at all. What difference should it make to Wolf Landau that the second son of the rabbi of Biala, Rabbi Menachem Mendel, had come from Poland on a visit to New York? What matter that Wolf was blood kin with Rabbi Manachem Mendel, and a great-grandson of the rabbi of Strykow? In Poland the kinsmen had never met. When Wolf arrived in New York as a sixteen-year-old boy, fifty-year-old Menachem Mendel had been a rabbi for years. He must be in his seventies now. And Wolf? The distance between the kinsmen was immense. Still, it often seemed to Wolf that he had been following in the footsteps of the rabbi of Strykow from the age of sixteen on. The Strykower had composed hymns of praise to God and the congregation of Israel; his great-grandson wrote poems to "girls like a half-moon."

Wolf's great-great-grandfather, Rabbi Abrahamel Ciechanower, had believed that defilement clings to one's finger tips at night, and since one's fingers are always likely to touch the face, the righteous Rabbi Abrahamel had slept in gloves. In deliberate reaction against his ancestor, Wolf dreamed about alluring girls and pig's knuckles. In essence, then, he too was preoccupied with the same "Other Side," with its nine and forty gates of defilement. So there was a connection of sorts between Wolf and his ancestors.

The moment Wolf Landau discovered that Rabbi Menachem Mendel was in New York, he grew restless. He mentioned it to no one, neither his wife nor his two children. Instead he tried to push the news item away, to persuade himself that he had shaken off the old days years ago. But the moment he was alone, he saw in his mind's eye an old man, six feet tall, with a "glorious-bearded countenance," dressed in silk and satin. Beard and earlocks were a blend of white. The eyes shone like bright Sabbath night candles. This, Wolf had been told, had been the image of the rabbi of Strykow, and the image of the rabbi of Biala. This had been the image of his great-grandfather, Rabbi Raphael. And this, in all probability, was the image of Rabbi Menachem Mendel.

As for himself, Wolf Landau had no trace of beard or earlocks. A shock of blonde hair fell over his forehead, trailing into his blue, dreamy eyes. A contemptuous smile for all human beings lurked in the corners of his mouth—contempt for the world, the smile of Oscar Wilde when sentenced to prison for sodomy.

Often, as Wolf stood before the mirror combing his wild shock of hair, he would ask himself: "What connection can there be between my smile of contempt and the rabbis of Ciechanow, of Strykow, and of Biala?"

On the surface there was no connection at all. But deep in his soul Wolf was drawn to the Ciechanower's simplicity, to his profound integrity. The Ciechanower used to say: "My forefathers could hide from people. But I, Abraham, am more sinful than they. Ever since my youth, I have been pursued by people."

For years Wolf had been working on a poem about his Ciechanower grandfather. The first stanza was always in his heart. Whether at home, or in the office, or in the street, everywhere he went, the verse manifested itself, insistent:

> *"You are nearest to my*
> *Blood, O Ciechanower!*
> *For me, as for you,*
> *Life is obligation."*

Whenever these lines forced their way into his consciousness, he perceived that he had been deceiving himself these twenty years; all his poems

about "nightingales blue and red" were mere butterflies on whose tenuous wings he tried to flee from
his ancestors. But, in reality, he was always crying:

"I am not free! A long chain stretches from my
forefathers to me!"

It was this ancestral chain that drew Wolf to
the chasidic rabbi who had just arrived from Pol-
and, to Rabbi Menachem Mendel, who, it was said,
had written sacred poetry in his youth.

Later that afternoon, Wolf got off the subway
at the East Broadway station on the Lower East
Side of New York. He turned down Henry Street.
As he did so, his heart seemed to rise to his mouth,
fluttering, restless.

The rabbi had established residence in a
wooden, two-story private home. He occupied the
entire second floor.

Slowly and cautiously, Wolf climbed up the
creaky wooden steps; he had no idea what he would
say to the rabbi. He remembered stories about his
great-great-grandmother, the wife of the rabbi of
Ciechanow, the righteous Ittele. Had she really
been so small? And when she went out in the dead
of winter to take a glass of preserves to some poor,
pregnant woman, had her grown sons really carried
their small mother in their arms through the waist-
high snow?

Coatless, his prayer vest showing, beard and
earlocks flying, a Jew greeted Wolf with the traditional interrogation:

"What good tidings do you bring?"

"Is Rabbi Menachem Mendel in?"

"Yes."

"Who are you, his sexton?"

"Yes."

"I would like to see the rabbi."

"Not on the Sabbath! He receives no one on the Sabbath."

"But it is not yet Sabbath."

"It is for the rabbi."

"Tell the rabbi a relative has come to see him."

"You mean, you are a grandson of Rabbi Wolf Strykower?"

Wolf nodded.

"Have you been in America long?"

"Twenty years."

"What are you, a business man?"

"No, I work for a newspaper."

"You're a writer?" the sexton pronounced the words with slow deprecation.

At that moment a door opened, and the rabbi, a tall, slightly stooped man stepped out in soft, felt slippers. The white socks above his slippers presented a blinding contrast to his black satin frock coat. A thick silk sash was bound loosely around his waist. An intelligent, wrinkled face framed by a pointed, gray beard looked at Wolf, pitying the poor man who marred the image of God with his modern dress.

"Sholom aleichem," said the rabbi. "I gather you are a grandson of Uncle Mottel."

"Yes, Rabbi."

"Your father told me he had a son in America. Your name is Wolf, isn't it, after the Strykower, of blessed memory? Your great-grandfather was a great man, Wolf."

"My great-great-grandfather was a still greater man," Wolf replied.

"Then you study?" the rabbi asked him.

"It has been a long time since I studied, Rabbi."

"That is shameful, Wolf." The rabbi's face clouded over. "However, the very fact that you, a writer, came to see me, a relative who is a rabbi, shows that you have not lost interest altogether. I am confident that you will return to the study of the Torah. And now, Wolf, it is Sabbath for me," the rabbi proffered Wolf his fingertips, and, humming the old Ciechanow melody, went into his room, shutting the door behind him.

Wolf remained standing in the middle of the room, looking at the closed door. Did he feel insulted? No. Who knew better than he how holy the Sabbath was to the Ciechanow seed! Rabbi Abrahamel Ciechanower had begged his fellow chasidic rabbis not to visit him on the Sabbath. If they did, he should have to behave like a chasidic rabbi, while he had always celebrated the Sabbath in the "ashkenazic manner."

And Rabbi Menachem Mendel? For him it was Sabbath already. Yet on this Sabbath the rabbi had come out of his room to greet Wolf, had spoken a few words, and then had returned to his privacy, humming the same Ciechanow melody that had been in Wolf's bones since his childhood.

That melody brought back to Wolf a vision of the first rabbi of Ciechanow, Rabbi Abrahamel, hastening immediately after Friday morning prayers from shop to shop, his sexton at his side, and checking the scales to make sure that Jews were giving an honest weight. And at two o'clock on Friday afternoons the sexton was already out by himself, striding through the streets and lanes of Ciechanow calling people to afternoon and Sabbath evening prayers in the synagogue.

As Wolf descended the stairs, as he walked down Henry Street, the melody of the Ciechanow Sabbath hymn, the words of *All those who properly sanctify the Sabbath,* returned to him; tenderly, he bore it through the streets of New York.

A Bratzlaver Chasid

At midnight the Warsaw-Kiev train began to approach the Polish border. The third-class cars, which had left Warsaw packed, were almost empty now. There were only three passengers in the last car. Two of them lay on the lower benches, heads thrown to the side, arms outspread, as though dead. The third passenger, a deep-chested individual with a sparse, blond beard, looked like a Russian peasant. Lightly, he jumped down from an upper bench, dragging a bag after him, out of which rolled a loaf of black bread and a tin of honey. The two sleeping passengers awoke, looked at one another, and asked the third man:

"What, are we at the border already?"

The third man did not answer; he did not seem to have heard or understood the question. Absorbed in what he was doing, he repacked the bread and honey and retied the bag. His fellow passengers agreed out loud that their companion was deaf and dumb. Turning their heads to the wall, they fell asleep again. Not until then did the deaf-mute open the car window; he put out his head for a moment, then pulled it back in. It was raining. The rain drummed on the roof, splattering against the panes.

The deaf-mute picked up the bag by its straps and threw it over his shoulder. Quietly, he left the car. He stood on the steps of the running board. The rain and wind blowing through the fields assailed him, but he stood motionless for a while. When his eyes had penetrated the darkness and his body had caught the vibrations of the chugging locomotive, the wheels biting into the rails, and the pounding rain, the deaf-mute climbed up the iron ladder to the wagon roof. For a moment he considered whether to remain on this car or to move on to another. A door scraped; the deaf-mute stretched out on his stomach and lay flat against the roof. The rain beat harder, the darkness thickened. The wind blew away every sound, the rain drenched every view. The deaf-mute had not expected the night to be so bad. He saw it as an act of God.

Going uphill, the train slowed. In the darkness, tongues of flame appeared, indicating the Polish border. The locomotive whistle shrilled, and the train screeched to a halt.

The deaf-mute's ears were so wide open and alert that he could distinguish in the rain and wind the merest scraping of a door, the lightest footstep. Nor was this to be wondered at. This was Wolf's twentieth illegal crossing of the border in the guise of a deaf-mute. Every Rosh Hashanah the Chasid made the trip to Uman to the grave of his former master, Rabbi Nachman of Bratzlav. He traveled with neither passport nor visa. Together with bread and honey, the bag over his shoulder contained a

volume of Rabbi Nachman's famous folk tales. He
was certain in his heart that his rabbi had not really
died—he was riding in the train with him. It was as
though the rabbi had merely changed cars; one had
only to call out—and he would hear. The journey
from Warsaw to Uman was a difficult one—as difficult as "the throes of the grave." Moving from car
to car in mid-journey, always fighting, always taking chances, Wolf's life was constantly in danger—
both on the Polish and the Soviet sides of the border. Nevertheless, not once in the nineteen years
since Rabbi Nachman's death had Wolf failed to
visit his master's grave in Uman. This was the twentieth trip. Up to this point the journey had been
fairly easy. God Himself was on his side. What a
rain, what a wind, what darkness! Is the passport
check over?

The locomotive shrieked. The cars lurched
sideways. The rain lashed at Wolf's wet feet and
drenched shoulders; the roof was too slippery for
him to sit down. Wolf crept over to the iron ladder
and stood under the roof, holding tight to the wet
railing. Shutting his eyes, he pressed his lips, and
wordlessly, soundlessly, recited some of Rabbi
Nachman's sayings. The urgency to reach Uman
and be received by the rabbi at his grave—this was
sufficient motive to keep Wolf warm. He no longer
felt his feet soaking up water like a blotter, no
longer feared to be pulled off the moving train at
any moment. Joy rose in his breast, as though he
were making a pilgrimage to Jerusalem. It was not
as if he were undergoing a complete spiritual ref-

ormation—that was not the cause of this joy. Rather, he was happy because it was a sufficient achievement for a human being to lift up one shoulder toward heaven—and the rain, the darkness, the danger disappeared. Because man, after all, was created to raise up heaven. Otherwise, it would have been impossible for Rabbi Nachman to be sitting inside the car while his disciple, Wolf, stood on the roof. The Soviet border already?

Wolf fell prone. But this time he did not stay on the roof of the last car. Pushing his bag ahead of him to wipe a path through the wetness, he crept forward over the car roofs.

At the fourth car from the locomotive, Wolf stopped. There was no iron ladder on this car; no one would take the trouble to crawl up to the roof to check. The wind, blowing from the field and forest, angrily flung sheets of rain at him.

Wolf heard the passengers leave the cars and move toward customs. There, after their baggage and passports had been checked, they would transfer to a Russian train for Kharkov.

Not he. Wolf would remain lying on the roof of the Polish train, until the station lamps were extinguished and the railroad attendants left. Then he would descend, and set forth through the wood to Shepetovka.

The locomotive began chugging again; smoke issuing from the chimneys sprayed the wet air with sparks. The train switched rails, moved on into the fields, and there stopped. It grew silent after a while. The only sound was the beating of the rain, the groaning and whistling wind. Then the Russian train departed.

Wolf had reached the roof of the last car. Light on his feet as a cat, the forty-year-old Chasid dropped down from the roof and lay under the car. He considered a moment the alternative of taking the highway toward Shepetovka, then thought better of it and decided on the fields. He crawled some two hundred feet on hands and knees, then straightened up. His arms and legs creaked as he began to walk. Yet, soaked through and through though he was, a warm glow entered his heart: he was to spend Rosh Hashanah with Rabbi Nachman's followers in Uman for the twentieth time.

Wolf passed through a field where the potatoes were dug up. There were small holes in the ground, mounds of dirt and puddles of water everywhere he put his feet. The night was full of rain and din; it was hard to tell where the noise was coming from. Suddenly, a dog started to bark. Wolf stood stock still. When the barking stopped, he moved on, to trudge, out of breath, toward the smithy that stood at the entry to Shepetovka.

Wolf knocked at the smithy window, then at the door. He heard steps, a voice:

"Who is it?"

"It is me, Wolf."

"From Warsaw?"

"Yes, Mendel."

A lock creaked open. The door opened; Wolf was struck by the warmth of the hearth. The two men greeted one another in the darkness, embracing. Thus standing, words were exchanged.

"Was it a hard journey?"

"This was an easy one. When do we go to Uman to visit the rabbi?"

"Tomorrow, if you wish."

The two men had a short drink in the darkness. Hastily, news was exchanged, tidings of the rabbi's Chasidim in Warsaw, Berdishev, and Uman. When the smith's wife went into the kitchen to sleep, both men got into the warm bed and immediately fell asleep.

A Rabbi

The rabbi's courtroom was in a state of neglect. Against the walls, peeling as though after a rash, stood bookcases filled with sacred volumes, piles of books. Here and there throughout the room, candle ends were stuck in dripping candlesticks and inkwells. On the rectangular table lay an open Talmud, surrounded by sheets of paper covered with minute letters in the medieval Hebrew script of Rashi. And on the Talmud lay a pair of bare, thin hands. Above the hands loomed a large head. A satin skullcap had slipped off the head, and lay on the table, sweaty mouth up.

It was afternoon.

Seventy-year-old Rabbi Mendel of the Men of Poland Synagogue was working on his magnum opus. The letters issued from his pen, tiny, well-formed, arching. Writing was a wearisome task for the rabbi, for one's mind cannot always sparkle. The fact that he had been a rabbi for some fifty years, and that he had gone through the entire Talmud three dozen times—of what consequence was that now? When one's mind stops sparkling, one feels oneself terribly small, unable to sit quietly at the table; one wanders from one bookcase to another.

Pulling books off the shelves, the rabbi leafed through them in desultory fashion. His mind soared above the letters, carrying him back to Plotsk, where he had served for thirty years. He recalled his former comrades, both those rabbis who had gone to their final rest in the world of truth and those who were still alive in Poland and America. With what self-assurance they had been wont to greet him then! Not the assurance that goes with genuine independence—a level only rare individuals can achieve. Rather it was satisfaction with self, pride of position, a low level of being indeed, that asserted itself.

Leafing aimlessly through the volumes wearied Rabbi Mendel. He took another volume of the Talmud and sat down at the table. The seventy years he had lived showed themselves in his emaciated body. One of his shoulders was higher than the other; one corner of his beard was ragged. He looked like a tipped scale.

Through the open window the Men of Poland Synagogue was visible. Was he really its rabbi? He began to doubt even that now. Somehow he could not believe that the plaster Shield of David that had replaced a cross had turned the former church into a synagogue.

Reverend Burke, the priest, had given him the church for a song. The priest had not wanted the church to be converted into stores. It pleased Reverend Burke, who had studied the Jewish Bible, that the people of the Book would keep God's house off the auction block.

When had all this happened?

Not quite twenty years back. In the course of that period, the Jews had moved into the neighborhood, and almost all the Germans had left. Where private residences had once been, now stood apartment buildings four and five stories high. Each apartment house was a miniature town, a settlement of some twenty or thirty families. At the time it had seemed as though people were digging in for the duration. Nothing less than a catastrophe could evict them. Yet all at once, on the High Holy Days of 1938, the Men of Poland Synagogue was almost empty. A year later, a delegation of Portuguese visited the rabbi:

Up till now the Lord had been praised in the language of the Bible. From now on, let him be worshipped in Latin. Let not the house of God remain empty.

Placing his hands on the open volume of the Talmud before him, and laying his head on his hands, Rabbi Mendel dozed. Sunbeams pouring through the open windows warmed his large head and closed eyes. There was a buzzing in his head.

"Who is it?"

"I."

"Reverend Burke?"

"Yes, Rabbi Graubard. Are you continuing the repairs?"

"We must be finished by Rosh Hashanah."

"You bought your house of prayer very cheap."

"Repairs are costly. . . ."

"It could have been sold for another five thousand dollars."

"The business men would have turned it into stores."

"That is why I made sure it was given to your people."

The priest took out a small snuffbox. Both men sniffed.

"Things are not good, Rabbi Graubard, things are not good. Men are sinful, are disinterested in faith."

"They certainly are not interested in faith here in America."

"Do you think that with all this prosperity people live any better? Believe me, they do not! The twenty Christian families still living in the neighborhood should have kept up the church."

"Things are no better among us Jews."

"Things are not good, Rabbi Graubard, things are not good. They would have turned the church into a shopping center. Man has surrendered completely to the devil. Yes. . . ." The priest put the open snuffbox to his nostril. "I am translating the Letter of Aristeas from the Greek."

"Whose letter?"

"Aristeas' letter, where he tells how the Bible was translated into Greek in Alexandria. I am translating the letter from the Greek, not from the Hebrew original. Rabbi Graubard, would you be kind enough to check several passages in the Hebrew?"

"There is no Hebrew text."

"None?"

"None."

The ringing of the doorbell spread through the courtroom. The rabbi raised his head and began to rub his eyes. He tried to remember his dream but he could not. He caught sight of his skullcap lying on the table. Hastily he put it on, glancing around to see whether anyone was looking; it was as though he had committed a transgression in allowing his head to be uncovered inadvertantly.

There was a louder ring. For a moment the rabbi stood motionless in the middle of the room. His eyes rolled; slowly the sleep-filled knees bent, barely able to carry the old, weary body. He shuffled to the door and opened it. In the doorway stood two respectable Negroes, wearing glasses.

They spoke their piece. It is this way, Rabbi Graubard. . . . God's house should not be empty. The Negroes followed the rabbi into the courtroom. "We know that the Portuguese have offered five hundred dollars more than we have—as though this is a piece of real estate and not the house of God."

It took the rabbi some time to understand. But when he gathered what it was they wanted, he stationed himself between the two Negroes, arms outspread.

"Neighbors, if it's a question of business, you must talk to the president of the congregation, not me. But I maintain that so long as one dozen Jews

still come to pray here, this must remain a synagogue."

After he had accompanied the two Negroes to
the door, Rabbi Mendel returned to the courtroom.
His sad eyes swept over the bookcases. At the sight
of the gold-trimmed book spines, he felt relieved.

There was a knock at the door, followed by
the doorbell. In the doorway stood an elderly Jewish woman.

"What is it?"

"I need your help, Rabbi."

"A question of kashruth?"

"Yes, Rabbi." She handed him a plate of duck
intestines.

Rabbi Mendel took the plate and went over to
the window. With a knife, he cut off a speck the
size of a blister, then a second one. He returned the
plate to the woman.

"Kosher."

Rabbi Mendel sat down again before the open
Talmud, before the sheets of paper with his minute
script. His mind began sparkling again. His glance
fell on a blood-specked ten-cent piece that the
woman had left on the table for him.

Rationalists

It was the first Sabbath in June.

In the courtyard of the rich man's house, the curtains stirred in the open windows, sending a secret message to the trim garden paths flanked on either side by large, rounded stones. The trim arbor, covered with climbing vines, where the military camp band played in the late afternoon on Saturday and Sunday, now stood empty.

Everything napped that Sabbath afternoon: the blooming cheery trees, the raspberry bushes, the three-story house. And in their beds, the master and mistress of the household napped, the children napped, the servants napped.

Only Tanchum, a tall lad of sixteen, engaged to a girl in Cracow, listened for a long time to make sure that his father and mother, brothers and sisters were really asleep. When he was sure that the entire household was napping, he slipped out of bed, took his felt, rubber-soled shoes in his hand, and slipped out the open door in his stocking feet. Passing through the corridor, he walked up two floors to the third story, where his teacher, Ludwig Levinson, occupied a large room with two windows. From the

windows one could make out the new marketplace
—and a piece of grassy field where a small church
stood among old, leafy oak trees.

The teacher, Ludwig Levinson, looked much
younger than his thirty-six years. His broad shoulders, long, thick mustache, blonde hair, and blue
eyes, all were reminiscent of a Polish country
squire.

Master Israel Alter was a very rich man, the
biggest purveyor in the province of Plotsk; he built
army camps, roads, the fortress of Modlin. He had
so distinguished himself that the governor presented
him with a gold sword which hung in the room
where he received government officials, a room
whose walls were decorated in dark blue velvet.

Master Israel Alter, with his abbreviated frock
coat and top hat, was also a follower of the chasidic
rabbi of Alexander. Summoning the teacher, then
an employee of the Warsaw community, to an
audience in the Hotel Polski, Master Israel Alter
spoke as follows:

"Mister Levinson, so long as you are a teacher
in my house, you are not to instruct anyone else.
You will teach my sons, young and old, Russian,
Polish, German, and a smattering of the Holy
Tongue—enough for them to be able to write let-
ters in the Holy Tongue to their future in-laws.

"Be very careful, *Panye* Levinson. I do not ask
you whether you are an observant Jew or a Rationalist. And you, for your part, are not to try to convert my children into Rationalists, the way Rationalists do. In particular, you are not to talk to them

about religion. Do you promise, *Panye* Levinson?"

"Yes, I promise."

"Give me your hand."

That was in the year 1880, a year and a half before this Sabbath afternoon. Ludwig Levinson had kept his word for a full year.

Levinson instructed his students every day, winter and summer. Lessons over, he strolled down the Wolker road from Mlawa to the railroad station.

In the evenings, he sat in his room writing a comedy. He was certain that his comedy would transform the lives of Jews in Poland. Levinson was not going to poke fun at the chasidic rebbes, with their courts and foolish adherents. He was not going to tear things down, to make a biting onslaught, to exaggerate the misconceptions and poverty of Jewish life. Rather, he was approaching the Polish Jews like a good-natured grandfather, a kindly uncle. He would laugh with, not at, his people. It would be a holy laughter, infectious, sweeping all who heard it off their feet. Every Chasid would laugh with him, and take his laughter into the benighted prayer rooms. Thence it would flow out into the streets where all folk, kith and kin, would join in the healthy, cleansing laughter.

Thus dreaming, Levinson worked through the winter and summer, till it was spring again.

The house of Alter was delighted with the new teacher. In the course of the year the sons had learned to read and write letters in four languages —Russian, Polish, German, and the Holy Tongue.

The house of Alter raised Levinson's wages. In addition, gifts were showered on him: now it was a silver cigar-holder, now a watch with Swiss works.

But Levinson was not pleased with himself. He was stuck in the fourth act and could not finish the comedy. The reason for this, he argued, was because life was too easy in the home of the rich Master Israel Alter. Nor was that all. In a certain sense, he had sold out. Never to speak about religion—or rationalism—what did that mean? Had he, Levinson the Rationalist, consented to *that?* Life was taking its revenge on him, for an easy life does not go hand in hand with breadth of vision if one wishes to change the world.

One spring afternoon, after lessons, Levinson detained tall, quiet Tanchum. He took him up to his room, supposedly to review the Hebrew letter that Tanchum had written to his in-laws in Cracow. As they talked, one word led to another, and the teacher discovered that all winter long Tanchum had been studying the *Guide to the Perplexed,* and was now studying the *Guide to the Perplexed of Our Age.* His teacher? A young man from Ciechanow, one David Opatowski, married to the daughter of a Mlawa family, an adherent of the rabbi of Kotsk. David was supposed to be instructing Tanchum in the Talmud. Actually, the young man had introduced Tanchum to works of criticism, with the aim of demonstrating that one can and must be a Rationalist as well as a Chasid. Rabbi Simcha Bunem was just such a combination, as was the rabbi of Kotsk, both of whom had beaten down the

Joseph Perls and Isaac Erters of their day, as had Maimonides himself, and Rabbi Lipman Yom Tov of Prague.

Levinson made the acquaintance of David, who for years had been boarding at his in-laws. Hours on end he studied Talmud and pored over critical works, writing poems in honor of the "Holy Jew," the rabbi of Pszisha, and the rabbi of Kotsk.

Every Sabbath after the big noon meal, when the house of Alter was asleep, David, taking a side street, slipped into Levinson's room. There they discussed the religious and secular books they had read, Levinson read aloud from his comedy, *Women's Knots,* and David recited his poetry from memory. Young Tanchum listened in delight.

It was the first Sabbath in June.

When Tanchum put on his felt slippers in the corridor and began climbing up the wooden stairs, his father, Master Israel Alter, stirred in his sleep. His ear caught the sound of footsteps. Who was walking about outside? He left his bed and inspected the bedrooms. The boys—Moshe, Hersh, Joseph, Shaye—all were asleep. But what about Tanchum, his ablest son? Where was Tanchum?

Hastily, Master Israel put on his silk dressing gown, the sash tassels dragging on the floor. He climbed up to the teacher's room on the third floor. Standing before the door, he listened:

Who was that speaking? It was not the teacher, nor Tanchum. Yet the voice was familiar. Might it be the young man who was teaching Tanchum Talmud? Ah, what was he saying?

"And I tell you, Levinson, that one cannot compare the Rationalists, the modern Erters and Perls, with the Jewish scholars of the Middle Ages. Nor am I speaking from a critical point of view, of matters of faith. Merely examine the works of Rabbi Joseph Arama and Rabbi Joseph Albo, who believed in Revelation. But even the sages of the Middle Ages who were free-thinkers faithfully observed the practical commandments. This was one of the main reasons for the survival of the people of Israel in the Diaspora."

"So, he has fooled me, the beardless one!" Master Israel Alter trembled with rage. He opened the door. "Why aren't you asleep, Tanchum? As for you, Levinson, you gave me your promise that you would not talk to my children about religion. You can pack up this evening. Because tomorrow you are going back to Warsaw. One's word should be as good as his bond."

As Tanchum left his teacher's room, his father followed after, slamming the door with an emphatic rich man's bang.

Simchat Torah

The golden days set in, the season of the festival of Simchat Torah, when the sun warms but does not scorch, and wild geese rise aloft in the autumn haze to fly honking to warmer lands.

Simchat Torah.

In the small Gerer synagogue where ten-year-old Joseph worshipped with his father, the Chasidim formed in groups after the Simchat Torah festive meal and left to gladden their hearts with wine. Those who had rich kinfolk washed down roast geese and duck in foreign wines. Those who were keen of mind visited the homes of the most influential and eldest of the Chasidim, where, between one melody and the next, between one dance and the next, there were learned discussions in the style of the Rebbe.

Only Joseph's father, David, a tall man in his late twenties, remained at home. Though David worshipped in the chasidic synagogue, he had no dealings with the Chasidim—nor they with him. Under their breath they insisted that David was a covert Rationalist, who ought to be expelled from the synagogue. But they did not expel him. This was not because David was a man of learning, somewhat of a cabalist, to whom one appealed for help in interpreting a particularly difficult teaching of chasidism from the school of Pszisha or Kotsk. Rather, what was important was that David's grandfather, Master Favesh Shraga, had supported Rabbi Mendel Tomashover, and that David's father, Master Israel Leizer, an old adherent of the Rabbi of Kotsk and one of the first followers of the Rabbi of Ger, was highly respected by the learned author of the *Sefas Emes*. Who would wish to bring shame upon Master Israel Leizer, lay his soul desolate, and shatter his heart?

David sat at a table strewn with holy volumes. He had just finished the last reading in the Book of Deuteronomy, which begins with the verse "This is the blessing wherewith Moses blessed the children of Israel" and had immediately gone on to the first reading in Genesis, "In the beginning God created." Now it occurred to him that the death of Moses was not really the end; it was a new beginning, it was Genesis.

This thought pulled him out of his chair. Thrusting a thumb under his sash, he paced the room, humming the tune of the hymn beginning, "Bridegroom of Genesis," which he had just been teaching his ten-year-old son, Joseph. David had a curly blond beard. His green eyes, the shade of water plants, were hazy. There was such a melancholy in his pacing and humming that if someone had rapped on the window pane—"David, what are you doing at home on Simchat Torah? Come, and rejoice with us!"—he would not have hesitated a second, but would have gone out immediately.

Ten-year-old Joseph sat at the window. The boy was unhappy, pained because his father was so strict. Weekdays, early in the morning when it was still dark, Father was already studying. Business came after prayer. On the Sabbath and holidays, Father sat over the holy volume night and day. No one from the little snyagogue ever came to visit him, nor did he go to visit them.

Joseph looked out the window—not a friend was in sight. They had all gone out with their fathers. Every now and then snatches of a lively tune issued from the wide courtyard where the wagoners sat in "Big-Bones'" tavern, singing:

"Whatever we may do, Jews is what we are."

The boy was fascinated by the singing. The words called to him: "Even the wagoners are enjoying Simchat Torah. They are sitting at table over glasses of beer and platters of fruit, while your father stays all alone, humming, as though he were not a proper Jew."

The father sensed his son's unhappiness and took him by the chin:

"What are you doing sitting at home, Joseph? Why don't you go out into the street for a while?"

"Where am I to go?" the boy burst forth. "Everybody else is with his father—but you always sit at home, even on Simchat Torah."

David felt guilty. He smiled and said:

"Very well. Do you want to go out? Come now, we'll go somewhere together!"

The lump in Joseph's throat melted. Delighted, he touched all the objects on the ledge of the open window. Seeing the ethrog case, he remembered that the children would be making torches tonight, and he pulled out the hemp.

A company of the older children who were too grown-up to carry flags like the small fry gathered in the synagogue courtyard. One boy held a hollow turnip that had been stuffed with hemp. He soaked the hemp in kerosene, then waved the turnip like a torch. Sparks flashed here and there as other boys set fire to wax candles with spurts from bottles of kerosene. Still other boys sprinkled the tips of broken matches on burning candles, then blew until the match heads lit up with a crackle, like Bengal lights.

The tumult in the courtyard increased. Elderly Chasidim danced in a circle, their sashes around their hips. Younger men whirled, their sashes flying, as the song pealed to the sky:

> *"Although, although, although Israel is desolated*
> *Still, still, still. . . ."*

Rising above the fires, the singing expelled the melancholy that autumn, harbinger of the coming winter, had laid upon the shoulders of Jews. Carried away by the lights and singing, Joseph forgot all about his father, who accompanied several Chasidim to Master Bunem's wine cellar. The latter was a great-grandson of the Preacher of Koszhnitz, and so thin with constant fasting that he was nicknamed "The Last Breath."

A group of Chasidim were going from one synagogue to another. They stood in the middle of the courtyard, and soon a new melody interrupted the first. Other Chasidim joined in; legs wove a dance:

"Ah, ah, ah,
With Thy command-ments, sanctify us."

At Master Bunem the winemaker's there was much drinking and talking of Torah. There was also a tacit agreement to make that personage David drunk, so as to discover once and for all whether the silent one was really a heretic. After his second glass of mead mixed with whisky and beer, David could no longer keep his chair, and stretched out on a sofa.

Samuel-David the slaughterer, one of the most respected Chasidim of Ger, whose preparations for prayer took twice or three times as long as the prayer itself, went over to David:

"Well, young man, what do you think? Was the Torah revealed on Mount Sinai?"

"On Mount Sinai." Hazily, David gathered what was happening and murmured, "Although, although, although. . . ."

"The lad is in his cups," someone cried.

"Go away, let me alone," Samuel-David the slaughterer would allow no one to come near. "What has happened to you? Your grandfather,

God rest his soul, was close to the court of Kotsk,
your father is one of the household of the author of
Sefas Emes—and you David, why are you never to
be seen in Ger?"

"Although, although, although." David screwed
up his eyes and mumbled into the sofa.

Joseph entered. He saw his father, pale-faced,
and was terrified.

"What's the matter, Father? Aren't you feeling
well?"

"He'll sleep it off, nothing will happen to him."

"It doesn't matter, today is Simchat Torah!"

David opened his eyes, and gave Joseph a lost,
apologetic look. "It's all for your sake, my son."

Suddenly David rose from the sofa. Laying
both hands on his son's narrow shoulders, he stam-
mered:

"Listen, Joseph, they think I'm drunk. You
know, son, they wanted to put me over the barrel,
thinking when wine comes in, the secret comes out.
Well, what are you standing here for, Joseph?" He
began to clap his hands. "Today is Simchat Torah.
We have finished 'And Moses died there,' and now
we must begin from the beginning all over again
with Genesis. Sing, Joseph, sing, boy:

> *"And still another virtue*
> *Hath Thy people Israel."*

Joseph could not look at his father, was unable
to understand what had happened. His father—
usually so quiet, so reserved, never agitated—now
all at once this way! Could they have made him

drunk? The boy could have thrown himself at the Chasidim who were standing around making fun of his father.

The cloud that had hung over David, the melancholy that had been lifted by the wine, flooded his brain again. His tall body tottered; he looked so pitifully sad that the boy burst into tears:

"Come, Father, come home."

Ten-year-old Joseph led his father home. And in the cool, dark Simchat Torah night a hoarse voice kept insisting:

> *"And oh, another virtue,*
> *Still another virtue,*
> *Hath Thy people Israel.*
> *Oh, oh, oh. . . ."*

Meyer Balaban

An open automobile twisted its way through heaps of bricks, past ruins where fragments of walls stood here and there.

The June afternoon air was filled with smoke and the stench of decaying matter. The smoke rose from the smoldering ruins; the stench from the mounds of corpses lying about the fallen houses.

The auto turned down Gensia Street into Smocza, down Smocza to Dzika, down Dzika to Bonifraterska.

A month before, these had been streets bordering on the wall of the Warsaw Ghetto. Now, there were neither streets, nor wall, nor people. At every turn one came across smoking rubble, as though after a fiery, all-swallowing earthquake.

The auto stopped.

Hans Wurzel, the curator of the Jewish library and museum objects, was the first to leave the auto. After him came Professor Meyer Balaban.

Fifteen years before, Hans Wurzel, a Polanized German from Lodz, had studied history under the renowned Professor Balaban. Wurzel at the time bore the Polish name of Wierszinski. Wiers-

zinski stayed on at the university after his gradua-
tion, as a lecturer in history. He paid frequent visits
to Balaban.

Immediately after the fall of Poland, Wierszinski turned into an "ethnic German"—that is, a
person of German descent living in foreign territory
who had never severed his ties with the homeland.
He became Hans Wurzel again, and broke with all
his Polish friends and acquaintances—all, that is,
except for the Jewish Professor Balaban, of all
people. And when Wurzel was appointed supervisor
of the confiscated Jewish libraries and museum objects, he assigned Balaban to the work of sorting
and classifying the material. Balaban was also preparing a German monograph for Wurzel on "The
History of the Jews in Warsaw."

Thus it went for a year. Though Wurzel was
Balaban's superior, they maintained the relationship
of a professor to a student who had surpassed him.
Suddenly, there was a drastic change in their relations. Balaban stopped being a mere messenger boy;
he became a cursed *Jude,* a Jew silently carrying
out the orders of his German master.

Hans Wurzel, walking ahead, was pointing out
what had happened to the Warsaw Ghetto to the
Jewish historian, once his mentor, then his subordi-
nate, and now his servant.

Thus it was that Titus had led Josephus
through the ruins of Jerusalem. But Titus, feeling
guilty, had continually apologized to Josephus. It
was not *he* who had ordered the Holy Temple
burned to the ground. In comradely fashion, Titus
had asked Josephus whether there was anything he

wanted saved from the ruins. Josephus had requested seven Torah Scrolls and seven Jewish prisoners; Titus had munificently granted Josephus seventy Torah Scrolls and seventy Jewish prisoners.

But Wurzel did not ask Balaban what he wished preserved; nor did Balaban make any request.

Walking through the ruins, past the dead, they did not speak to one another.

Except once. As they were about to turn from Dzika Street into Bonifraterska, Wurzel stopped Balaban, who was barely crawling along, his torn shoes tied crudely with strings. They were standing in front of a collapsed wall, where a worn velvet tallith bag hung under a black, rectangular mark. Wurzel pointed to the mark:

"What is that?"

"A 'momento of the destruction.'"

"The destruction of Jerusalem?"

It was hard to tell whether or not Balaban answered. His face remained impassive. Wurzel did not repeat his question. He said angrily:

"What progress are you making on the monograph?"

"I have written three-fourths of the book."

"I want you to write a final chapter—'The Fall of the Warsaw Ghetto.'" Wurzel pointed to the ruins, speaking deliberately, and watching for the effect his demand would make on the professor.

The words fell into the furrows and wrinkles of Balaban's face, producing no discernible change. He answered calmly:

"I shall write it, Herr Wurzel."

"How long will it take you?"

"Three days."

"What is today—Wednesday?" Wurzel ticked off the days on his fingers. "Thursday, Friday, Saturday. . . . You have three days. You are to read the chapter aloud in the Belvedere on Saturday evening."

"Yes, Herr Wurzel."

"And you are to avoid sentimentality," Wurzel commanded. "You yourself used to insist that a good historian must keep to the facts, not allow himself to be misled by emotion. An historian, you used to argue, needs a good eye and a keen nose. So look hard at the ruins, smell the corpses—more eye and nose, and less heart—you understand, *Jude?*"

"Yes, Herr Wurzel."

On their return from the ruins, they were silent again. But the trip was a short one. Soon the auto stopped. As Balaban stepped out and turned to shut the car door, it slammed in his face; the auto raced furiously away. Balaban's heart pounded; half-dead with sheer terror, the professor walked through a gateway, then down what was once a luxurious hallway, but now was damp, cold, and dark as a cellar.

Balaban lacked the strength to climb the four floors, and sat down on the first step. His swollen feet were heavy and pained him. Untying the shoe strings and loosening the shoe tongue, he relaxed all over—heart, eyes, and face.

Suddenly a hot lump stuck in Balaban's throat —the Jews had been slaughtered, murdered. Their houses were leveled to the ground. Only one Jew was left—Meyer Balaban; and he was required to see it all. He could not endure it.

Balaban covered his face with his hands. He burst into tears of self-recrimination:

"Why didn't I cry when I stood on the ruins of the ghetto? Why didn't I cry at the sight of the martyrs' bodies strewn among the ruins? Why didn't I recite the Mourner's Prayer?"

His weeping grew louder. He dragged himself, thus weeping, up the four flights, and entered his apartment, where the bookcases against the walls were packed with hundreds, thousands of books.

He called his wife by her Jewish name: "Gittel, Gittel!" He called his daughter, his two sons. But no one answered him. His wife and daughter had perished. His sons? Had they died during the ghetto battles? He did not know.

He lay down in his clothes on the torn ottoman. A cloud of dust rose. Before long he fell asleep. He slept some twelve hours.

When Balaban awoke, it was late in the day. Opening his eyes, he looked about him in amazement, as though at another world, far off, where everything was unfamiliar.

A warming sun ray touched him on the forehead, disentangling the threads of his memory. He was borne back to the outskirts of Lemberg, where he had lived as a child with his grandfather and father.

It was the eve of Shevuot.

His grandfather was patting him on the head and cheeks:

"Come, little Meyer, let us go to town to visit the Old Synagogue. Today is the anniversary of the martyrs, Rabbi Chayim and Rabbi Joshua Reizes, who were burned to death in the marketplace some two hundred years ago."

At ten, Meyer knew the story. The rabbi of Lemberg and his younger brother had persuaded an apostate to return to Judaism. For this, the brothers Reizes had been imprisoned and condemned to a horrible death. First, their hands and feet were to be chopped off. Then, their tongues would be torn out of their mouths. Finally, they would be quartered and burned to death.

Rabbi Joshua cut his own throat on hearing the verdict. The elder brother, Rabbi Chayim, was promised every advantage if he would allow himself to be converted. He refused to listen. He had but one request of the murderers: "Torture me one hour longer, but do not shave my beard off before I die."

On Shevuot eve Rabbi Chayim of Lemberg was taken to the scaffold where the executioner stood ready with the axe in front of the blazing fire. Rabbi Chayim turned to the weeping Jews of Lemberg and said:

"Do not weep, Jews. I have earned this punishment, which is from God. My hands deserve to be cut off, because my father-in-law bought me the rabbinate of Lemberg. My tongue deserves to be ripped out of my mouth, because I studied and con-

versed with priests in the Latin tongue. But I do
have one last request. On my tombstone let the
words be inscribed: 'And the whole house of Israel
shall lament the burning that the Lord hath
burned.'"

Little Meyer and his grandfather had reached
the town, were in the street of the Serbs, approaching the well where the martyrs had been burned to
death.

Meyer could hear the wild cries of the mob,
the crackling of the flames, the screams of Rabbi
Chayim under torture. He huddled closer to his
grandfather:

"Grandfather, would you have the strength to
die, like Rabbi Chayim, for the sanctification of the
name of God?"

"I?" Grandfather stood near the well, reflect-
ing.

Little Meyer did not wait for the reply. At ten
years of age he felt that *he* would be strong enough
to undergo martyrdom.

That martyrdom had occurred in the year 1686.
And now?

Balaban rose from the ottoman and stood at
the open window.

The reflection of sunrise filled the early morning. Silence clung to the old, gray walls. Above the
silence a frozen scream hung in the air—the scream
of slaughtered Jews, of the leveled ghetto. Where
are you, Gittel? And you, my sons—Alexander,
Leibel? And my only daughter—where is she?

Balaban washed the tips of his fingers. Then he

took the prayer shawl, unfolded and examined it, and slowly recited the words:

"And just as I cover myself with this prayer shawl in this world, so may my soul be deemed worthy of being clothed in a prayer shawl in the hereafter...."

There was a flashing in his temples; his heart was on fire. Somewhere in the distance a weeping face shone:

"Mama, Mama. Little Meyer will not write the final chapter of the history of the Jews in Warsaw. ... Little Meyer will not read that chapter in the Belvedere ... Mama, Mama. ... Something of his great-great-grandfather has survived in little Meyer —Rabbi Leibush, the president of the community of Lemberg, the 'lion that breathed revenge' who refused to be intimidated by the governor of the province, by the state itself. ... Something has survived in little Meyer of Rabbi Chayim Reizes, the burning bush that burns and is not consumed."

Meyer Balaban thrust the prayer shawl away, letting it fall to the floor. He stood at the open window, where the dawn moved over roofs and turrets. The expanse gathered into his mind, and there was no room for thought.

Balaban stretched out his arms, stretched out his body. The rooftops came to meet him. Faster, faster. To his ears came sounds, to his eyes flames. The seven and sixty years of his life tore themselves loose from the weary body, and burst into another life that burns and is never consumed.

Four Hundred Years

In the botanical gardens a crow cawed. The cry was taken up—soon the whole flock was cawing. The effect was an eerie one. Then suddenly there was silence again—a silence so complete one could hear early evening arrive with the new moon.

Betty awoke.

The December sky—blue and empty—and the snowy, naked botanical gardens peered into her bedroom.

Betty remained lying on the ottoman, hands under her head, legs crossed. Her brain tried to make sense of the patches of light sweeping over the waxed floor and playing hide and seek on the walls. She missed the transition from daylight to evening which she had skipped in her sleep.

Betty searched for that transition period with her closed eyes, and was disconsolate at not being able to find it. Her mood turned from regret to melancholy—the deep melancholy of a woman who has passed the threshold of thirty.

Nothing nowadays pleased Betty—neither Columbia University, where she was taking courses in philosophy, nor the art academy where she studied painting and sculpture—no, not even her husband with his real estate holdings and his love of her.

What matter that she had been living with this man for eight years, was attached to him, missed him when he went traveling? What was she to do with this voice that constantly cried within her, that she bore like a hump on her shoulders, this urgent voice demanding night and day, this voice that complained that she was a woman of thirty, and was still childless?

The hunger for a child swept through every part of Betty's body. It reminded her constantly that century after century the Caros had mortified their bodies, disaccustomed them to food, made their bodies flexible as an arrow, that, light and airy, they might laugh at the wind, laugh at the storm, and soar from land to land. Betty's great-great-grand-father—a great-grandson of the renowned Rabbi Joseph Caro—had been imported to Poland by a Jewish community. One of her grandfathers, Dr. Moses Caro, was the rabbi of a Reform congrega-tion. Betty's own father, however, was a secularist. And Betty herself had no beliefs at all. Generations ago the Caro family had changed its outlook on life. Nevertheless, they all bore children. So far as family continuity was concerned, her socialist father agreed with the Cracow rabbi and with his great-grandfather. But Betty was an only child. Her cousin, Joseph, the last Caro to bear the name, had never married. . . . And was there at last to be nothing left of great-grandfather, nothing left of grandfather, nothing left of father—nothing left of the Caro name at all?

Betty rose from the ottoman. She removed the bone hairpins from her hair, and the loosely gathered braids fell over her shoulders. Putting on the light, she stood near the switch for a moment, expectantly. The black hair and black eyebrows, thin and arched, emphasized the pallor of her long, dark, and lovely face; her dark eyes squinted, unable to bear the sudden light.

Betty tied her braids above her head as though to clear her eyes, and swaying, confident, moved on slender legs to the telephone table. She dialed.

"Hello—is that you, Joe?"

"Yes. Who is this?"

"Betty. Betty Caro Baker. Your cousin—you remember?"

"Why, hello, Betty! Of course, I recognize your voice now."

"Listen, Joe, how about coming over here today?"

"Who is going to be there?"

"Nobody. Morton is away. He's in Florida."

"What time do you want me?"

"Make it at eight."

"O.K., Betty, I'll see you then."

Betty hung up the receiver and sat at the table thinking.

How long had it been? Three years ago, five, eight? Joe—or Joseph as she had called him then—Joseph came up to the mountain resort where Betty's parents were staying. To the right of the red-roofed bungalow was a ripe plum tree, mown meadows full of sun, flowers, fruit. To the left ran the waters of the Neversink River, coiling and winding within its narrow banks, so cool and refreshing in the evening. He was twenty-five at the time, she twenty-two. Both were young, both hungry. They tried to still their hunger with Otto Weininger, with D. H. Lawrence. Then all at once, it was as though the blinders had been removed from their eyes. There was so much sun, so many flowers, the fruit was ripe, and the summer—and they in the middle, Betty and Joseph, twenty-five and twenty-two. Greedy years, never to be satiated.

Sun-ripened days, golden twilights. There was only one word in Betty's vocabulary: Joseph. It was a name whose combinations and permutations encompassed her entire world. That summer Betty thought with the tips of her fingers constantly running through Joseph's hair; she thought with her ever-thirsty lips.

But the Caro brothers—Betty's father and Joseph's—were opposed to the match. They were fearful that the children of the marriage of first cousins might turn out to be sleep-walkers or imbeciles. In addition, there was a volume of the Mishnah belonging to Rabbi Joseph Caro that had been passed down as a family heirloom. The frontispiece contained the following inscription in medieval Hebrew type:

"Eat little, drink little, never lose your temper. Never be of a haughty mind. When you hear malicious gossip, press your lips together like a millstone and be silent. So long as your health is good, keep no servants; for the servant, too,

was created in the image of God. There is no higher commandment than to die a martyr's death for the sanctification of the name of God."

Betty knew that this aspiration to die a martyr's death had its origin in an ancestor of hers who had come from Safed. That longing had accompanied the Caro family in its migrations all over the world. Now only two descendants remained—Joseph and she.

Her parents had quickly talked Betty out of marriage with Joseph and found her a rich husband. Paradoxically, there had been no issue at all from this marriage—not even a sleep-walker.

Joseph had never married. He continued his studies at Columbia, where he experimented with flies. His dream was to evolve a new species; but he continually carried his experiments to the point where the flies degenerated, stopped reproducing completely.

Betty rose from the telephone chair and began to dress.

At the stroke of eight Joseph arrived.

Under his black eyes and on his lips lay the fatigue one sees in people who are habitually short of sleep. His sparse black hair covered a bald spot on the crown of his head.

Shaking hands, the cousins regarded one another silently. Betty sat on the ottoman, and bade her guest join her.

"What is the weather like? Is it cold? Tea will be served soon."

"Thank you, but I would prefer to walk. I've been cooped up in the lab all day."

Betty, preoccupied with her own thoughts, did not hear Joseph's reply. She pulled her black silk dress down over her knees, and suddenly asked, with a very serious expression:

"How long is it since we last met?"

"Two years."

"You have changed, Joe."

"Why, have I grown older?"

"I don't know about that, but you look very tired. Do you really work so hard?"

"But you, Betty, are prettier than ever!" For the first time, Joseph looked carefully at his cousin.

Betty served Joseph a cup of tea. She placed her white, soft hands, with the long fingers extended, on a black velvet pillow, as though for a manicure. She sat silently for a long time, then, lifting her hands, clasped them sadly.

"You know, Joe, last night our great-grandfather came to me in a dream." She pointed to the wall where the portrait of Rabbi Solomon of Cracow hung. "That was the first time he ever appeared in any of my dreams. . . . I was amazed in my sleep that we could communicate. All at once, I knew how to speak Yiddish. He was unhappy because the family line is dying out with us. You are a bachelor, Joe, and I . . . I have no children. . . . With us, he said, four hundred years of the Caro family comes to an end. . . . Then I woke up and could not go back to sleep. And all day I have been feeling so sad. I just had to call you up."

"You need a child, Betty." When it was too late, Joseph wished he could withdraw the words. Unable to do so, he fumbled with his tea cup.

"So do you, Joe!" Betty's black eyes glistened.

"Oh no, I don't need a child." Joseph moved the cup away abruptly. "Not I. I don't believe in dreams, and I am not impressed by pedigree. What is the importance of four hundred years of the Caro line? A biological experiment . . . that has to end sometime . . . if not with my father and yours, then with me and with you, Betty."

"Not with me!"

Betty changed the subject. "You say it's not too cold for a walk?"

"Fine weather for a walk. Shall we go?"

"Yes, let's go. By all means!" She rose and put on her fur coat.

The evening was cold and snowy. They went into the botanical gardens, where the snow lay on the green fir trees, between the trees, and the air, dry and cold, made one's step more brisk, one's feet firmer.

Miracles

Twenty-three-year-old Rabbi Jacob was in an exuberant frame of mind. The eminent Rabbi David of Prague had entertained him royally. Wines and meats such as these Rabbi Jacob had never tasted before. Wealth? Silver, gold, crystal, beggaring description. And the rare collection of sacred volumes: first editions, parchment manuscripts, scrolls with silver clasps. The finest Jews in town, the elite of Prague, had been invited for the dinner in Rabbi Jacob's honor. All evening, the rabbi had held Rabbi Jacob's hand, embracing him like a son. Rabbi David of Prague repeated and reiterated the praises of Rabbi Jacob's father, the author of the *Chacham Zevi*. One did not see geniuses of that sort nowadays. Rabbi Jacob's father had been one of a kind.

The laudatory words warmed twenty-three-year-old Jacob as much as did the wines, the meats, the words of learning at the table. He trembled, remembering the delicious odors he had carried out into the street with him, hugging to himself the rabbi's caress, the warmth of his fingers, the ring of his voice.

At first glance, Rabbi Jacob did not seem as old as twenty-three. The long, pallid face, suppressing inner fires, was sprinkled with the sparse, curly hair of a fifteen-year-old boy. The yellow peaked hat Jacob was required to wear in Prague made his narrow shoulders still more narrow. He was as tall and thin as a drawn arrow.

The evening was well advanced. The ghetto shops were about to close, as were the streets, lanes, alleys. Night began to fall. The first lights flickered in windows, indicating the presence of narrow brick buildings. The Talmud melody flowed into the street from the city's two yeshivas where students fervently chanted.

Rabbi Jacob noted an elderly Jew walking behind him. He stopped. His follower stopped, too, and motioned Rabbi Jacob to walk on. Rabbi Jacob asked:

"What is it you wish, master?"

"The rabbi sent me to show you the way home."

"You need not trouble." Rabbi Jacob thrust a coin into his hand.

Rabbi Jacob had been in Prague for over a week. After his father had died, leaving his wife a widow with small children, Jacob, as the eldest, had journeyed to Germany and England to claim the debts due his father. He took along copies of his father's books to sell. Rabbi Jacob struggled through the world for some two years. At the end of that time he had collected none of his father's debts, sold but few of his father's books. On his way back to Moravia, where his wife and two children were

awaiting him, he had stopped over at Prague; here
his father's books were detained at customs.

In Prague Jacob was staying with his uncle
Wolf, a cabalist who bought up white wool at mar-
ket fairs. This wool, which came from Hungary,
Wolf exported to Hamburg.

A monk in black entered from a side street
and walked straight toward Rabbi Jacob. Rabbi
Jacob did not step aside, and the monk passed silently by. When he had gone some distance, Rabbi
Jacob dared to stop and look back at the monk,
disappearing into the night; he marveled at his own
audacity. A Jew was liable to punishment in Prague
if he did not step aside for a Christian ecclesiastic.

Rabbi Jacob disliked Prague. At every turn
one encountered monks, priests, seminary students.
All of them wore black. All of them persecuted the
Jews. The monk's willingness to overlook Rabbi
Jacob's crime was a good omen. In fact the whole
day had been full of miracles.

This very morning his books had been returned to him in customs. When they were first confiscated, his uncle had bade him apply to Rabbi
Jonathan. He, the son of the author of the *Chacham
Zevi* apply to Rabbi Jonathan? No, never. Later,
Rabbi Jonathan himself had informed Uncle Wolf
that if Rabbi Jacob were to apply to Eibeschutz
personally, he would have the books released from
customs. Rabbi Jacob did not go to Eibeschutz, and
the books had been released *without* his intervention. To cap it all off, when the books did arrive, the

finest Jews in Prague had come to Rabbi Jacob's stall, and had bought them, paying cash.

Rabbi Jacob entered a narrow building. The steps, coiling like an earlock, led to the home of his uncle Wolf. At the door he was reminded that his uncle and aunt had gone off to the fair, leaving behind their youngest daughter, Sarah. Widowed a year after her marriage, Sarah made Rabbi Jacob uncomfortable with her attentions.

In high spirits, Rabbi Jacob entered with a hearty good evening. Sarah, a pretty and lissome version of her kinsman, came to meet him with an air of assumed anger:

"Where have you been so late?"

"The dinner at the rabbi's has just ended."

"Many people there?"

"Of course."

"You know we are alone, Jacob?" Sarah took his hand in hers. "Papa and Mama won't be back from the fair until tomorrow."

He recoiled. The young blood flooded his arms and legs, his hands and temples. For a moment he allowed her to hold his hand in hers, but his eyes and face pleaded with his kinswoman:

"What are you doing, Sarah?"

"I love you," she raised her eyes and lips to him, and pressed her cheek against his.

"We are sinning, Sarah." Stroking her hand gently, he began to slip away, at a loss for words, to the room he occupied.

"Are you going to sleep so soon?"

"Yes, Sarah. I have been running about all day and am tired."

"Shall I fetch you your usual bedtime drink?"

"A glass of tea? If it is not too much trouble." Rabbi Jacob hesitated, then said: "I've drunk so much wine today I'll be able to sleep without the tea. Good night, Sarah."

As he lay in bed on a downy mattress, and with a downy cover over him, Rabbi Jacob took out his diary. There, by the light of a candle, he wrote in rabbinical Hebrew:

"Today a miracle occurred to me such as occurred to Joseph the righteous. Perhaps an even greater miracle—for I am a hot-blooded young man, and have been away from home for a long time. The Evil Inclination will not let me be. I was left alone with a beautiful young woman, my kinswoman. And she is so forward and shows me so much love. She *almost* kissed me. When I lie in bed, she comes into the room to cover me—supposedly as a kinswoman should. If I were to heed the Evil Inclination, my kinswoman, for love of me, would do anything I asked; I have often thought I could be seduced. The spark need but lick the flax to burst into flame. But I overcame my Evil Inclination, though it held me tight in its arms. I overcame it with the help of God. May the Master of the Universe guard me and my children from the flame of the Evil Inclination and fire of Gehenna."

Rabbi Jacob laid his diary under his pillow, snuffed out the candle, and with a deep sigh sank between the downy covers. A day of miracles, indeed.

The Mute Hungarian

In the swamp of Stupsk, a three-hour drive from Mlawa by ox cart, a band of partisans made their camp.

It was a small band, ten in all, consisting of two families: the ranger Kviatek and his four sons, and the ox-trader Lemel and his three sons. A stranger had joined them, a mute Hungarian, who looked more like a giant mountain peasant than a Jew.

For years the two families had lived next door to one another in a clearing in the forest near the border separating the Polish state forest from the Prussian one. Both families engaged in hunting and smuggling. They went nowhere without a rifle or revolver—the eternal enemy of the plow. Speaking little, they kept their distance from the neighborhood peasants and the border Jews, whom they regarded with suspicion as competitors.

The two families got along. Both Kviatek the ranger and Lemel the ox-trader were men of daring. They were both resourceful. Both made out well—with sons like theirs to help, great things could be done. But suddenly—calamity, total disaster. The

Germans took away their oxen, took away their cows and horses. When the womenfolk refused to tell where the men were hiding, they were all shot; the houses were burned to the ground.

The band took its revenge. First the commander of the garrison at Wolka was shot—next, the commander at Stupsk. They blew up the Wolka railroad station; then the Mlawa water mill, which ground rye and wheat for the Germans. German night patrols disappeared, or were found shot to death.

The revenge was so drastic that the enemy could not believe that it was the work of a mere half-score of partisans. At the slightest suspicion, villages were burned, old men and children hanged.

The Germans proclaimed a reward of 10,000 marks for whoever brought in the ranger Kviatek or the ox-trader Lemel, dead or alive.

But they were not brought in, though many a peasant in the border villages knew where they were hiding. On the contrary, the villages provided the partisans with food, supplied them with bullets, hand grenades, detonation mines. And the peasants told the partisans the whereabouts of the enemy.

Two years passed.

It was the beginning of December. For the second successive day a dry snow had fallen. Cold winds lifted layers of snow and broke them against the trees and stumps, which looked at a distance like white bears. It was late afternoon. Lemel's youngest son, Samson, was standing watch, rifle in hand, guarding the entry to the partisan hide-out in the Stupsk swamp. The wind carried a muffled sound to his ears. Extending one leg, Samson listened, every muscle of his body alert. He could see no one; he heard only the beating of his own heart in the silence. Was it Polish? Germans had often trapped Jews in this manner. No, it was not Polish. Samson moved into the late afternoon. Was someone praying? It grew silent again He heard nothing, but could sense the enemy moving on every side. They could slip out behind him from every tree. The swamp, the wood, everything urged: "Throw away your rifle! Run back to the barracks! Tell them we're encircled by the enemy!"

Samson was all eyes, but he could see nothing. Suddenly, from behind a snowy bush a huge, broad giant of a man appeared. He did not look like a Jew, he was not a German, he was not a Pole. He spoke not a word, but the expression on his bearded face was so fearful that Samson's arms and legs grew weak. He raised his rifle in terror and shouted: "Put up your hands!"

The stranger placed his hands on his head. Samson shouted:

"Walk!"

He led the stranger through the swamp to the partisan camp.

The newcomer was suspect. Kviatek untied a sack from the man's shoulders and opened it. He pulled out a loaf of bread. Then he dug further and said to the ox-trader:

"He seems to be one of yours, Lemel."

He held up a bag containing a prayer shawl

and phylacteries. But it was some time late at night before the man could convince the band that he was indeed a Jew. In mute show he told them that he had come from somewhere in the Carpathians, that he had escaped from Auschwitz, where his wife and children had been burned to death, and where Jews were being exterminated by the trainful.

The man stayed with the partisans. He became one of the pillars of the group. They called him "the Hungarian." At dawn, while all the partisans but the man on watch were still asleep, the mute Hungarian stood outdoors in his prayer shawl and phylacteries, praying. He threw his arms around a snow-covered tree, as one embraces an eastern wall in the synagogue. Enveloped in the prayer shawl, his head lay on his arms, the broad shoulders writhing. The frosty early morning was filled with pain:

"O Father, Father . . . Father in heaven. . . . Help. . . ."

"Who is that talking?" Kviatek sprang up from his rude bed.

"Who is it?" Lemel went to the door and listened.

"The stranger must be a holy man," declared Kviatek.

Everyone believed that to be so. Everyone agreed that he was not a real mute, but had taken a vow never to speak. Who knew the heaviness in this man's heart? He was one of the first to go out and track down the enemy. It was he who had come back to camp twice in one week with a live German tied to his shoulders like a bound calf. And then, he knew how to cure frostbite, how to pull teeth.

A month passed.

The band learned that a freight train was due to arrive that Saturday after midnight—and it would *not* stop in Stupsk. It was carrying boxcars full of Jews from France and Italy to Auschwitz and Maidanek, to the gas chambers.

At midnight the band was dispersed around the entrance to the forest. Every man stood behind a tree. The bitter wind and frightful snow assailed them. Hands and feet were numb. But when the chugging of the locomotive was borne to their ears through the snow, they forgot cold and danger. Each raised his head to cast a glance at the track-man's booth, a hill of snow in the distance.

From the booth emerged a fur-covered track-man; he stopped and waved a green lantern:

"Everything is in order."

The chugging of the locomotive, the clatter of the wheels, the whistling of the wind—all sounds were twice as loud in the night, where the thick snow made it impossible to see.

The freight train pulled uphill with a last, desperate heave, as though about to collapse. The locomotive passed the trackman, pulling boxcar after boxcar.

The trackman extinguished the lantern and began walking back to the hut. Suddenly, he threw off the worn sheepskin and stood, six feet tall, in a white coat. He counted the cars:

"Four, five . . . eight . . . ten. . . ."

He jumped on the steps of the last boxcar. The train was still pulling uphill. The mute Hungarian's ears were wide open; he could detect the slightest scratching sound, the lightest step, in the uproar of wind and snow.

The mute Hungarian crawled along the roofs of the boxcars toward the engine. Wind and snow whipped his face, his shoulders. He clung to the car roofs; his eyes were shut, his lips were tight, praying silently, like Samson: "Let me die with the Philistines!" And when he arrived at the first car, joy surged up in him. He took two hand grenades from his belt and flung them, one after another, into the locomotive. Tongues of fire flared to the sky, lighting up the snow and the wind. The locomotive reared, pulling the first car with the German soldiers off the tracks. Explosion after explosion deafened his ears, hurling him out of consciousness. Only his lips moved, repeating the question:

"The Jews? . . . Saved?"

Wind and snow whistled in reply.

Pedigree

Poland, 1937.

The High Holy Days were over, and the Cysho* schools had reopened after the long summer vacation.

The school on Pietrokow Street was in a festive mood. The children were entertaining a visitor—Joseph Strahl from the United States, a writer whose works the children had read and studied. And here the author himself had unexpectedly appeared.

The children in the senior class—boys and girls from ten to twelve years old—sat in their Sabbath best. Their eyes—black, brown, and blue—were shining. Their faces glowed. The children were delighted at their visitor's accessibility. He was not sitting in the chair that had been specially set up for him in the front of the room—he preferred to sit on a middle bench, with the children round him. Soon, the children no longer considered Strahl a visitor. He had turned into a favorite teacher, one of those whom children fall in love with and cling to. He

* Central Yiddishe Shul Organisazie, a Bundist school.

told the children all about Isaac Leib Peretz and Sholom Aleichem, whose pictures hung on the walls, and who seemed to be listening with faint smiles to what Strahl was saying about them, delighted at the way the children were enthralled.

The visitor told the children about Jewish schools in the United States. When the class complained that both children had died in his story "The Judgment," Strahl apologized. The children also expressed their vexation at his story, "Solomon's Judgment," where Strahl did not present King Solomon as the wise and good man portrayed in the Book of Kings.

"Was King Solomon really such a man?" Strahl asked the class.

There was a moment of silence. Thirty pairs of eyes looked at Strahl in amazement; his question seemed to them unanswerable. A slender hand was raised. The teacher called out:

"Do you want to speak, Mirel?"

"Yes."

"Then you may." The teacher bent over to the visitor. "Is this girl a relative of yours? Her name is Strahl, too."

Mirel, whose head was barely visible in the group of children, lost her self-possession temporarily. Then, recovering, she coughed and said:

"I say that King Solomon was not really a good man."

"How do you arrive at that conclusion, Mirel?" asked the teacher.

"I arrive at that conclusion because of his son

Rehoboam." Mirel's dark eyes lit up. "Rehoboam said to the people of Judea: 'My father chastised you with whips, but I will chastise you with scorpions.'"

"Correct, correct!" Strahl was delighted. Little Mirel had eyes like his own, he thought, large and dark. "How old are you, Mirel?"

"My birthday is in December," Mirel replied. "I will be ten years old in December."

"Mirel is the youngest in the class," a boy called out.

"And how long have you been attending this school?" Strahl asked.

"A year."

"And you are in the senior class already?"

"I had already read all of my mother's books in Old Yiddish when I began school." Mirel's pious little face shone happily; she was not boasting, but simply relating a fact. "And I am the only one in class who can pray—I can even say the Sabbath prayers."

Strahl, the teacher, and the children, all laughed heartily. After he had said goodbye to the teacher and the class, Strahl went over to Mirel. He stroked her black hair:

"Mirel, what is your father's name?"

"Papa? David. They call him Master David the winemaker."

"He deals in wine?"

"He used to make wine for the Sabbath. But an innkeeper informed on him—if the little synagogue of Kotsk had not helped us, we would all have gone to prison."

"And what does he do now?"

"He teaches Talmud to young men."

"And he sends you to the Cysho school?"

"Mama sends me. Papa thinks I'm going to a cheder."

"Tell me where you live, Mirel, and I'll come visit you tomorrow morning."

"You don't have to go to all that trouble. Tell me where you are staying, and Papa will come to see you."

"The Hotel Polski."

"Do you really think we are related?" Mirel looked at Strahl with hopeful eyes. "I should so like to be related to you."

"Possibly we are, Mirel, possibly we are." Strahl stroked her head again. "Ask Papa to come to see me tomorrow morning."

Stepping out into noisy Pietrokow Street, Strahl took the first waiting taxi.

"Hotel Polski."

While attending a writers' congress in Paris, Joseph Strahl had made a side trip to his native Poland, where he had grown up in a city near the Prussian border. His father, David, who had died in New York, was originally from the town of Zdoynske Wolia. Strahl was en route thither, to visit the ancestral graveyard, when he had stopped off at Lodz. He knew that his grandfathers and great-grandfathers lay in the Zdoynske Wolia cemetery, and that some of his uncles and granduncles still lived in Zdoynske Wolia. Possibly, Mirel's father, Master David the winemaker, was a kinsman of his —named after the same great-grandfather David as Strahl's father.

Strahl shut his eyes. He was not troubled by the violent shaking of the taxi or the noise of Pietrokow Street. In his mind's eye he could see Jewish communities of old—Vienna, Prague, Posen, Lublin, Zdoynske Wolia.

Everywhere there was kin, everywhere learning and scholarly acumen. Before his shut eyes walked his grandfathers and uncles. Their faces were like heavy pages of Talmud, their eyes mirrors of wisdom and sadness. Little grandmother Mirel. Her bell-shaped hat was trimmed with silver filigree, like the crown of a prayer shawl. She was dressed in white silk. Grandmother was always busy attending to the needs of yeshivas, of poor women in labor, of widows, and of deserted wives. She was goodness itself. The same name as ten-year-old Mirel, who had read all of her mother's books in Old Yiddish. . . . The taxi stopped. They were at the Hotel Polski.

When Strahl awoke early the next morning, the streetcleaners were at work, and Lodz was humming with activity. Everywhere were trucks and wagons and people who hurried off to work, in street cars. The gray November air was filled with the shrieking of sirens, the clatter of horses, and human voices.

Strahl descended to the street to breakfast in a cafe that smelled of fresh bread and rolls. Then he

158

bought several newspapers and returned to the
hotel. As he approached the hotel, his heart
stopped. A tall man of about thirty-five was walking toward him—his blonde beard was curly, his
green, sad eyes were overcast. As he walked, he
murmured to himself. The sadness in that walk and
murmur caused every passerby to stop and look. "I
could swear that is my father!" Strahl cried in-
wardly. That was exactly how his father used to
walk almost every Sabbath after the Third Meal,
murmuring to himself as he paced from room to
room before Mother lit candles for the Sabbath's
end.

Stopping the stranger, Strahl offered his hand:
"Sholom aleichem, Master David Strahl!"

"Aleichem sholom," a pair of intelligent, sad
eyes smiled in response. "How did you come to stop
me, of all people, in this crowd?"

"You bear a strong resemblance to my father."

"Where does your father live?"

"My father is no longer alive. He was called
David, too, after his grandfather from Zdoynske
Wolia. His mother, my grandmother, was called
Mirel."

"I was born in Lodz, and am named after my
grandfather, who is buried in the old cemetery
here."

"Where was your grandfather born?"

"Grandfather?" the young man grasped his
beard with two fingers. "To tell the truth, I don't
know. At five I was orphaned. My mother married
again, and my stepfather used to laugh at my pedi-

gree; he boasted that *he* was descended from the
Preacher of Koszhnitz. I told him off, finally, when I
grew up: 'Stepfather, your lineage ends with you;
with me, David Strahl, it begins!' "

They both fell to laughing; looking into each
other's eyes they laughed heartily, not like complete
strangers, but like persons who are really very close,
have not seen each other for a long time, and now
have suddenly met. The young man shook his head,
his green eyes smiling sadly:

"The only pity is my little daughter, Mirel. She
was so happy to think that we are related. What am
I to tell her now?"

"Now," Strahl took a ten-dollar bill out of his
pocket, "you can tell her that Uncle Joseph left her
a goodbye gift."

The two men smiled, and parted. Strahl
watched Master David the winemaker walk away.

"Father's walk," he said to himself. "I could
have sworn it was Father."

The Chumash Lad

Day was breaking when five-year-old Yossele awoke. For a while he rubbed his eyes. Then he sat up and listened to his father, who was in the next room, review the Sabbath reading from the Bible with a melody of great sweetness. The tick-tock of the wall-clock provided a steady counterpoint to his father's melody. The melody and the ticking of the clock sounded loudly in the early Sabbath morning silence that hung in the air, caressing his eyelids and whispering that today was the Sabbath when the Consolation chapter from the Book of Isaiah was to be read—today Yossele was to become a Chumash lad and begin the study of the Five Books of Moses. The first reading from the Book of Leviticus began to run through his head; but he knew it almost by heart, and soon turned his attention to his speech.

Yossele flung himself out of bed, devoutly poured the morning water over his fingertips, and began to recite the *Modeh Ani*. Then he put on a freshly ironed shirt, a new prayer shawl to be worn under his jacket, and a pair of squeaky new boots which the cobbler had brought the day before. As he got into his new frock coat, he looked disdain-

fully at the old cap with its twisted visor. He knew
that a new velvet cap awaited him in the schoolroom. Only yesterday, his teacher, Master Pesach,
had written the words "Crown of the Torah" on a
shiny white tablet, which he had sewn on the brim
of the new velvet cap; today Yossele would put on
that Crown of the Torah cap when he delivered his
sermon.

With a cheerful "Good Sabbath, Papa," Yossele entered the dining room, where his father was
sitting at the open window reciting the Sabbath
reading.

"Good Sabbath, my son." The father embraced his only son. "Off to the schoolroom so
early! What about breakfast?"

"The rebbe has to review the reading and the
sermon with me, Papa." Yossele showed his father a
bound kerchief, within which lay two pieces of
white chalah smeared with fat, a chicken wing, a
piece of honey cake, and some cherries. "Mama
prepared this for me."

"Look here, Yossele . . ." His father pulled his
five-year-old son to him, and kissed him, unable to
finish the sentence.

In the street Yossele became aware that what
his father had wished to say was: "Look here, Yossele, see to it you don't shame me." No, Yossele was
determined not to shame his father and mother. He
ran through the empty streets, the Chumash reading
running through his head. As for the speech: he
knew it with all his body—not just his mouth, but
his arms, his legs, his eyes. Every part of his body
was full of joy and movement:

"Yossele Lipsky is becoming a Chumash boy today!"

The celebration was all prepared at the Lipsky home. The heavy pieces of furniture had been removed from the parlor. Five rows of chairs were set up for Yossele's schoolmates. There were two chairs at the head—the one on the right for Yossele, the one on the left for the "interrogator." Against one wall stood the square table with its wings extended and covered with a sparkling white table cloth. On the table stood a pitcher of red wine, a honey cake, a torte, and platters of nuts, dates, oranges, and cherries.

Father and Mother, Grandfather and Grandmother, aunts and uncles—all stood near the open windows facing the street and waited impatiently for the young folk to arrive. Suddenly there was a shouting:

"Here they come!"

First appeared the assistant teacher—tall and thin as a rail. Next came Yossele and his interrogator. Some twenty boys followed, two abreast. The teacher, Master Pesach, brought up the rear, smiling into his long beard, as though to say:

"My students give me nothing to be ashamed of!"

Yossele's velvet cap flaunted its Crown of Torah band, making him taller. Windows and doors opened. There was joy in every eye and face.

"Here comes Yossele, the Lipsky lad!"

"Happy the mother, happy the father who have lived to see this day! There's a fine lad for you—no evil eye! Black satin eyes!"

Near the Lipsky's three-story house the procession halted. The assistant teacher grabbed Yossele's hand:

"Come!"

He dragged Yossele up to the first story, opened the door, set him down as though he were a piece of furniture, and called out:

"Blessed are ye who come!"

The children burst into the house. The assistant seated them in five rows, four abreast. Yossele he placed in a chair on the right, the interrogator on the left.

All at once the living room turned silent. The children stared at the table groaning with so many delicacies. Father and Mother, Grandfather and Grandmother, and all the relatives, consumed Yossele with their happy eyes. As Yossele began his speech, his thin, bell-like voice pealing, the eyes of his mama, lovely Rachel, were flooded with tears. Yossele said:

"*Ani bar chacham*—I, a clever lad—*eftach pi* —Open my mouth—*le'emor divre chachamin*—to utter the words of the wise. For the Torah makes him who studies it wise, in accordance with the words of Scripture: *Ki hi chachmatchem u-vinatchem le'ene ha-amim*—for it is your wisdom and your understanding in the sight of the peoples. Ah, but if you should ask me how I, a small boy, dare to stand up and preach before such a holy congregation—the reply is, I have learned to do so from the saying: *Hechacham omer*—the sage says: *Ashre hador shehagedolim shomim min haketanim*—

happy is the generation whose grown-ups listen to the wise words of small children—and I certainly am a small child. Therefore, I beg you to listen to my words of Torah."

The audience applauded with delight. Master Pesach the teacher lifted his beard; a prolonged sound of disapproval issued from his lips. When silence was restored, the interrogator, a red-headed boy with clever green eyes, arrogantly bent over to Yossele:

"Come here, little boy."

"I am not a little boy any more."

"Then what are you?"

"I am a serious lad now."

"What makes you a serious lad?"

"I have, with God's help, begun to study the Chumash."

"So, you have, with God's help, begun to study the Chumash. Well, what does Chumash mean?"

"Chumash means one-fifth."

"One-fifth of what?"

"One-fifth of the five holy books of the Torah."

"Count the five holy books of the Torah on your fingers."

"Genesis, one, Exodus, two, Leviticus, three, Numbers, four, Deuteronomy, five."

"And which Chumash are you studying?"

Yossele showed his third finger.

"What, are you studying a finger?"

The children sitting on the chairs burst into laughter and waited eagerly for Yossele's reply. Yossele pushed his Crown of Torah cap back over his forehead, and answered with assurance: "I am not studying any finger. I am studying the third Chumash."

"Leviticus begins with the word 'Vayikra.' What does that mean?"

"Vayikra means 'and He called.' "

"Who called?"

"God called our master Moses and taught him the laws of sacrifices."

"Well, lad, recite the Chumash!" The interrogator pointed to the assistant, who immediately handed an open Chumash to Yossele.

Almost without looking and in his thin voice, Yossele chanted and translated the portion of *Vayikra.* And when he came to the word, *"U-lenetacheha"*—meaning "to its pieces"—he added: "May Papa and Mama cut big pieces of honey cake."

The small folk chimed in:

"Big pieces of honey cake!"

Father and Mother were walking about with the platters, serving honey cake and tarts. The gathering continued to celebrate noisily, and the assistant clapped his hands:

"Silence! The Chumash lad must finish his speech!"

All on fire, the five-year-old boy stood up on his chair and nervously tugged at his cap as he waited for quiet. He began:

"Ana mi-zera yosef ka'atina—I am one of the children of Joseph the righteous. Just as Jacob blessed his son Joseph the righteous, that no evil eye might befall him, may you too not give me an evil

eye. Rather than that, let Papa and Mama give the rebbe and the tutor a big sermon gift."

At these words the interrogator bent down to Yossele and said with disdain:

"They will certainly not give a lot of sermon money."

"They certainly *will* give a lot of sermon money."

The two boys fell into a furious hassle. Finally, the interrogator pretended to lose his temper, and gave Yossele a slap. Yossele became angry. Lowering his head, he said with a sulking mouth:

"Why have you humiliated me before the holy congregation?"

"My dear comrade, if I have humiliated you, *hate et roshcha ve-avarechecha*—lower your head and I will bless you."

Yossele bent his head. The red-headed boy laid his hands on Yossele's head and spoke to this effect:

"May the Name, Blessed be He, endow you with Methuselah's years, with the grace of Joseph the righteous, with the courage of brave Samson, with the wisdom of King Solomon, with the wealth of Rabbi Eliazer ben Charsomes. Children, all say Amen!"

"Amen and amen!" The entire audience large and small, burst out with such joy that the panes in the windows trembled. "Where is he, the Chumash lad, where is he? Let me kiss him!"

The celebration began.

The Eternal Wedding Dress

Dawn was breaking when eighty-year-old Glickche Schreiber opened her eyes with terror, immediately to shut them again.

Glickche was unable to move. It was as though every limb of her body were out of joint, the arms and legs separated from her hands and feet. There was a gnawing pain throughout her body; in the front of her mind lay the dream that had been wearying her all night long.

"Had Ernestine really died?"

It was only when Glickche opened her eyes again that she grasped the full truth: Ernestine had died Friday afternoon.

What else could they have done? Wait with the burial until Sunday, as is the custom in America? In Pressburg, where Glickche's parents and forefathers had lived, such things were done differently. The dead were buried on the day of death.

And then—it had been Friday afternoon. Ernestine had not provided herself in advance with a shroud. True, she was Glickche's blood cousin, an

Eiger, the grandchild of Rabbi Akiba Eiger. But
even fifty years ago in Pressburg, she was one of the
Reformed. Ernestine's angel (for everyone does
have a guardian angel in heaven) was deaf, even in
Pressburg. He never hearkened to her demands, so
that even in Pressburg she had gone astray. Take
her very name—Ernestine. They were both named
after the same grandmother, Glickche. But Glickche
became Ernestine. And what right had she to put on
airs, this Ernestine? Because her husband was an
eye specialist? Because she spoke Hungarian, German, French, and English? Glickche's husband was
a heart specialist; in fact, a professor in Budapest.
And here in New York he lectured at Columbia
University. And Glickche herself? Ever since they
were both children, she had been more talented in
languages than Ernestine. Besides, Glickche could
translate, from the Hebrew, the Five Books of
Moses and the Psalms. What right, then, had this
Ernestine to put on airs, to stray from the straight
and narrow? And she had died so improvidently,
without a shroud. There it was Friday, Friday afternoon in fact. What else could they have done?
Glickche had taken her own shroud and given it to
Ernestine as a present. They had returned from the
cemetery just in time to light the Sabbath candles.

Glickche saw evidence of God's loving-kind-
ness in this. She lifted her eyes in gratitude to
heaven:

"Father in heaven!"

Snatches of light drifted through the windows

overlooking Central Park and were reflected on the eastern wall, facing Jerusalem for prayer. The sunbeams lit up the faces on the wall. Glickche gazed at those bright faces, the age-old beards and earlocks, the clever eyes with their expression of sorrow. These were her grandparents: Rabbi Moshe Schreiber of Pressburg, and Rabbi Akiba Eiger of Posen.

The sight of her ancestors eased Glickche's mind. It was not only in Glickche that her ancestors were reflected, but also in her sons, specialists like their father, and Sabbath observers who did not write on the holy day. Her son-in-law, a rich factory owner, kept closed on the Sabbath. Every Friday evening one of Glickche's grandsons came to her home to chant the benediction over the Sabbath wine. The grandson would sleep over at his grandmother's, then accompany her to services the next morning. What of her sons and grandsons? Why, they deserved to have the gates of the Garden of Eden wide open for them merely because of the way they observed the commandment to honor their parents.

Glickche lamented the passing of her generation. Almost every year the ranks were thinned by the loss of a friend. And she had friends from the old days in Pressburg, as well as the sixty years she had been in New York. Now one by one the friends were departing for the world of truth.

Glickche began counting them on her fingers. Still left were: "Not Radish, not Freydche, not Sheyndel, not Breyndel, not Sarah. . . . How terrible!"

She counted some seven names. She saw the face of every one of her friends, and remembered their ages. The youngest was sixty, the oldest in her nineties.

In her mind's eye her friends were standing in a row. Glickche thought to herself:

"Whose turn is it next?"

She knew that it was not Freydche's. Ninety-year-old Freydche was something of an amateur doctor. There was nothing she could not cure! And when a person fell ill, long days in advance she could predict who was "destined to live" and who was "destined to die." As early as Wednesday she had known that Ernestine was dying. Glickche asked her:

"Freydche, how can you tell?"

Freydche replied:

"If you want to know whether a sickness is fatal, Glickche, take a piece of soft bread, smear sweat from the sick person's forehead on it, and throw it to a dog. If the dog eats the bread—good; if not, it's all over."

Glickche looked at Ernestine's black dog, refusing to leave the sick bed. The dog would not go near the piece of white bread that Freydche had thrown him.

Heaping curses on the dog's head, Glickche left Freydche in a rage. But the thought would not let her rest—Freydche had really guessed right. How, after all, did she do it? With magic?

The telephone on the table near Glickche's bed rang. Glickche picked up the receiver.

"Who is it? Radish? Good morning, Radish! God grant us no more sorrow! Will you be welcome? Of course, of course, a most welcome guest! But why so early? I'm still in bed. . . . I have not said my prayers yet. . . . Come after prayer. . . . Fine, that's fine, darling Radish!"

The old woman had forgotten how every part of her body hurt her in the morning, as though every limb were broken. She left the bed immediately and called her maid:

"Elizabeth, are you still asleep?"

"Who sleeps, Mrs. Schreiber?"

The maid, an elderly Negro with sorrow lurking in her eyes and at the corners of her lips, entered Glickche's room.

"Here I am, Ma'am."

"Be a good girl, Elizabeth, and tidy up the room."

"What's the hurry, Ma'am?"

"We're expecting guests."

The old lady lifted her shoulders in a childish gesture and smiled appealingly. By the time Elizabeth had finished the room, Glickche Schreiber was sitting near the eastern wall with her prayer book; her grandfathers' pictures hung on the wall over her head—the author of *Chasam Sofer* and Akiba Eiger.

She chanted a Pressburg melody as she prayed, loudly, unaware that the tune was being hummed wordlessly in the kitchen. There, Elizabeth was preparing breakfast.

Just as Glickche finished the Eighteen Benedictions, the doorbell rang. At the door stood

Radish, Freydche, Sheyndel, Breyndel, Sarah—all of Glickche's friends, wealthy old women of good family, holding in their hands boxes of cakes, bottles of wine, and sewing bags.

"Good morning, Glickche!"

"Good morning, Glickche!"

Amazed, Glickche kissed her friends. After they had sat down at the table, where the cakes were served and the wine bottles opened, Radish, the oldest of the group, took out a piece of Irish linen and spread it over the polished floor.

"Can you guess why we have come, Glickche? Your friends have come to sew an eternal wedding dress for you. You have well earned it, Glickche. You gave your own wedding dress to Ernestine, as a gift, and are left without one of your own. So we have come here today, on Sunday, to make you a new one."

There were tears in old Glickche's eyes. Without saying a word, she embraced each of her friends. Then she sliced a torte, and poured glasses of wine. Having eaten and drunk, Radish, the oldest, put a snood with points and bows on Glickche's head.

As the old women threaded their thin needles, pulled at the long white threads, and, bent over, began to sew the eternal wedding dress, Death began to spin his tune.

In the Jewish District of Vienna

After the Sabbath afternoon nap, the people of the Jewish district of Vienna began to gather in the synagogue courtyard. The first to appear were the artisans from the Street of the Dyers, the Street of the Skinners, and the Street of the Cobblers. They collected around the two smiths, the brothers Jacob and Meyer, both powerful men, who lived at the square, close by the stone tower. Their houses, which had survived the first expulsion of Jews from Vienna, were still called by their original names—Jacob's was "The House of the Green Wolf," Meyer's "The House of the Blue Wolf."

The two smiths worked on commissions for horse-traders, draymen, and iron founders. All week long, from early in the morning until late at night, they hammered and forged glowing bars. Long after the pitch torches had been extinguished in Vienna and it was totally dark outdoors, there was still light in the Jewish district. Yeshiva boys sat around flickering candles, studying, while the rest of the populace was asleep. Through the empty streets rang the clanging of glowing bars, proclaiming to the whole world the power and industry of the smith brothers. How pleasant it was to hear them; how fervently one studied then!

And, indeed, they were a remarkable pair, well worthy of note. There was one task the smiths had executed with such skill and dexterity that all of Vienna came to see and marvel, as at a rare wonder. From a wellspring under the earth they had tapped water that ran through copper pipes directly into Master Moshe Mireles' three-storied home. And the water flowed *up* from floor to floor.

The Jews were vastly proud of the smiths; they also highly esteemed Master Moshe Mireles, the pride of Vienna. Master Moshe Mireles—great in lineage, great in learning, great in wealth—was Vienna's link with the renowned communities of Ashkenaz, Bohemia, and Poland.

Dressed in their Sabbath best, on the steps of their homes sat grandmothers and mothers, reading Yiddish Bibles or eating Sabbath fruit. At the half-opened windows, black, blonde, and red heads of girls could be seen. The heads would disappear from time to time, but their youthful, ringing laughter lingered to peal through the quiet Sabbath afternoon.

Several score yeshiva boys arrived from the far-off Street of the Swords. From their dress it was apparent which of the boys hailed from Ashkenaz, which from Bohemia, which from Greater Poland. Walking in twos and threes, the boys entered the Large Synagogue, where the Genius of Pil, eighteen-year-old Rabbi Elikum Getz, was to deliver the guest sermon. The Genius was visiting his blood relation, Master Moshe Mireles, who lived in the Street of Paris.

The older yeshiva boys had prepared in anticipation of the sermon. As was the custom, they were sure that the Genius would intersperse his sermon with references to any number of talmudic tractates. He would challenge one difficult passage by reference to another still more difficult—and resolve the difficulty with such speed that it would be hard to grasp what he meant. The head of the yeshiva was to be at today's sermon; the next morning, Sunday, in the presence of the finest householders in town, he would order his students not merely to recapitulate the sermon, but to pose questions on it as well. And the lad who could raise the best questions would have an assured future, as the son-in-law of a rich man.

From the narrow streets and lanes where small wooden houses grimaced crookedly, the yeshiva boys turned off into the Street of Paris, leading to the synagogue courtyard.

In the Street of Paris practically all the houses were built of brick. The shops were barred with iron doors. Narrow, two- and three-story-high buildings with arched windows, forged iron doors, and peaked roofs, loomed over the Jewish district like watchmen. Here, where the Sabbath afternoon nap still reigned, boys were playing "Yours and Mine." An occasional girl was glimpsed moving behind the heavily draped windows.

There was a small park in the middle of the street, where gnarled apple and pear trees overlooked a wooden fence. Between the trees stood a sukkah, not yet completely dismantled after the Festival of Booths.

It was the beginning of the month of November, and leaves, dry and red, were strewn thickly between the trees. The blue, cold air resounded with the honking of wild geese, preparing to migrate to warm lands.

Here the yeshiva boys stopped this Sabbath afternoon on their way to the synagogue for the guest sermon, and stood by Master Moshe Mireles' park. Supposedly, they were enjoying the trees, plants, and fresh air. But the truth was they were basking in the reflected glory of Master Moshe Mireles' pedigree, his learning, his wealth. The very name was impressive: Master Moshe Mireles, of the lofty clan of Heller-Tumin-Frankel-Segal-Wallerstein.

Master Moshe Mireles had already married off his four daughters. Now, he himself occupied the second and third floors of his house, together with his small family—his wife and newly married daughter, Sarah. His son-in-law, Rabbi Isaac-Mayer-Tumin-Frankel, was Master Moshe's blood nephew. Soon after the wedding, Rabbi Isaac-Mayer had gotten it into his head that he must translate the entire Bible into Yiddish. When offered a writ of rabbinate, he had driven the messengers away, bidding them return when the translation was completed.

Master Moshe Mireles rented out the first floor of his house to a physician, Master Judah Loeb. On his door, fronting on the street, hung a tin placard inscribed in Latin:

LEO VINKLER, MEDICO HEBREO.

And in the reception room, where Master Judah Loeb received patients, a parchment diploma hung on the wall. The diploma informed all and sundry in cursive script that Leo Vinkler had, on the 22nd day of March, 1629, been graduated from two faculties in the University of Padua—that of medicine, and that of philosophy.

Dr. Vinkler, a learned man, wrote and spoke five languages—Hebrew, Yiddish, Latin, Italian, and German. Whenever it was necessary for the Jewish community of Vienna to be represented before the authorities, it was Dr. Vinkler who was dispatched. And when the Christian scholar Wagenseil came to Vienna, he always paid a visit to Dr. Vinkler in the Jewish district. The physician went about with Wagenseil's Hebrew letters, and Wagenseil went about with Dr. Vinkler's Latin letters.

The yeshiva boys were aware that Wagenseil had been the physician's guest for almost a week now. Wagenseil had been to the prayer service that morning in the Large Synagogue. He had sat up front with the physician, near the eastern wall, close to the Holy Ark. And, as the reader read from the Torah Scroll, Wagenseil quietly followed the reading in a Hebrew Bible. The Jews in the synagogue had been delighted.

At this moment, Master Moshe Mireles

emerged from his three-storied house. He was followed first by Dr. Vinkler and Johann Christophe Wagenseil. Behind them came the Genius of Pil, Rabbi Elikum Getz, and Master Moshe Mireles' son-in-law, Rabbi Isaac-Mayer.

It grew suddenly silent on the Street of Paris. The women sitting on the steps, the girls at the open windows, the small fry and the older children—all stood stock still in awe. With silent joy they gazed upon the five men as one gazes upon royalty.

"There they are!"

"Here they come!"

As Master Moshe Mireles turned into the synagogue courtyard, his servitor, an agile little man, sprang before him, the three-cornered hat on his head veering like a ship in the wind. He had a black goatee, and his worldly-wise eyes seemed to be in earnest conversation with the waving earlocks that flew ahead of him.

"The smiths of the city council have come to inspect our water pipes."

"By all means, Sabbatai, show them around." Master Moshe was pleased. "Take them into the cellar and show them the entire machinery. They fancy themselves important, these tin-smiths— they'll find there's something they can learn from our smiths, the brothers Jacob and Meyer."

Master Moshe Mireles had fallen back to talk with his servitor; now he hurried to catch up with the Genius of Pil. The latter, tall, thin, and slightly stooped like a well pole, was silent. He was deep in reverie, trying to decide whether to deliver the

sermon he had prepared, or a new one, one that
would be a reply to Wagenseil. At the home of the
physician, Master Judah Loeb, the Christian had
made merry at the expense of Rabbah bar bar Hanna,
with his whale, his sea creatures, his enchanted
ships. Wagenseil, who was planning to translate the
talmudic tractate, *Baba Bathra,* into German, intended to delete Rabbah's "exaggerations." The
audacity of the Gentile—he who could barely make
out a reading from the Five Books of Moses! The
presumption!

The Genius, who at the age of seventeen had
written a commentary on the legends in the Talmud, was up in arms on behalf of Rabbah bar bar
Hanna. The Genius had written in the introduction
to his volume *Rapduni Bitapuchim:* "Some people
mock us, saying that since the words of Rabbah bar
bar Hanna are pure fiction, the same holds true for
the entire system of the Talmud—which heaven
forfend! The truth is, Rabbah bar bar Hanna was
speaking in parables and enigmas, which require
explication and elucidation."

Nor was the Genius, Elikum Getz, the first to
have taken up the cudgels for Rabbah bar bar
Hanna. Famous rabbis before him had done so:
Solomon ben Meir, and Solomon ben Abraham
Adrat, and the Genius' own kinsman—the "Ma-
harsha."

Master Moshe Mireles inclined his head toward the Genius:

"Deep in thought, Elikum Getz?"

"We should not have been silent."

"You mean, with Wagenseil?"

"Yes. And I shall answer him in my guest sermon."

"The Viennese scholars will not be pleased."

"Then I will preach for them again, tomorrow, following the Afternoon Prayer."

Master Moshe Mireles did not reply. Taking the Genius by the arm, he ushered him into the synagogue.

The Large Synagogue was already packed. The pews were filled. People stood along the walls and around the wooden pillars. The poorly lit synagogue was even darker than usual. The wax candles on the platform and pulpit, burned down three-fourths of their length, cast shadows that thickened the darkness in the corners of the room and around the pillars.

A moment of silence. Then the crowd began pushing to get closer. There was a flustered whispering:

"Master Moshe Mireles."

"The physician."

"Who is the Gentile?"

"Wagenseil, one of the Gentile sages."

"A lover of Israel, 'tis reported."

"Which one is the Genius?"

"There he stands, on the platform."

"The one putting on his tallith?"

"Yes."

"He is so young!"

The sexton rapped on the table—once, twice, three times. The synagogue grew quiet, so very quiet one could hear the floorboards creak, hear the wax candles drip and sputter.

Eighteen-year-old Elikum Getz advanced to the pulpit. The prayer shawl lay over his thin, narrow shoulders, the skullcap on his head had moved down to the nape of his neck. He began by telling one of Rabbah bar bar Hanna's legends:

"Once upon a time a group of Jews were sailing on a ship. . . ." Unable to bear the yoke of wicked Rome any longer, a band of Jews had fled the Holy Land in a ship. For a long time the ship sailed on until it reached what seemed to be land in the shape of a fish covered with sand and plants. The Jews were certain they had arrived at Babylon, which because of its shape and its location between two rivers has been likened to a fish, its vegetation likened to date trees. They settled down, thinking they had found a second holy homeland, only to have their new Babylon overrun by Persians. The Persians, who worshipped fire, began to persecute the Jews. But they had really landed on a huge fish. Feeling the heat on its back, the fish turned over. Luckily, the Jews were able to save themselves by fleeing to their anchored ship; otherwise they would certainly have drowned. And ever since that time, the Jewish people have sailed the stormy seas in that same ship.

The face of the Genius had become pale and he breathed with difficulty. His narrow shoulders were raised, thin, like sharp arrows, pointing— pointing to the pain and courage displayed in Rabbah's legends, and to the greatness of this wandering scholar who had traversed seas and deserts, experienced and survived the wickedness of Babylon, the decline of the yeshivas in the Holy Land. Substitute the Babylonian captivity for the sea beasts and desert beasts in the legends of Rabbah bar bar Hanna, and their meaning becomes clear. In the words of the commentator and poet Ibn Ezra: "Some of them are like delicate silken threads, others like heavy burlap."

The Genius spoke on, citing one text after another, and the unplumbed depths of his knowledge opened. He raised objections only to resolve them, linking one idea with another, and that other with still a third. And as he spoke, his listeners became aware that that which remained still unspoken was even greater, a kind of supreme "Silent Observer," whose meaning was to be sought in the furrowed forehead, the deep eyes, the parted hands.

The Genius had left his audience far behind— no one could grasp his meaning. Yet they listened with bated breath as the words rushed from his lips. Before their eyes, a mystical leap to divinity was taking place. The words were throwing bridges across rivers, weaving and forging secret forces. Light spread through their hearts, exultation; for there was a Genius in the synagogue, one who spoke the words of God, here, near the stone wall where the strong smiths dwelled.

Suddenly—a groan. Flinging up his thin white hands in ecstasy, the Genius had overturned a candlestick. The candle lay burning near the old Ark curtain.

"Do something about it!"

"What can we do?"

There was a stirring in the half-dark synagogue:

"Call the Sabbath Gentile!"

"He isn't there!"

Dr. Vinkler inclined toward his guest, Wagenseil, and whispered in his ear.

Johann Christophe Wagenseil, in his fine knee pants, black fur cape and stovepipe hat, went up to the platform. With two fingers he lifted the candle, replaced it, and modestly returned to his pew.

Glowing eyes, glowing faces, followed his movements, wordlessly thanking him, regretting that so learned a man was a Gentile, that he had acted the part of a Sabbath Gentile.

And the Genius?

The prayer shawl lay on his shoulders, the skull cap on the nape of his neck.

The white hands, racing to capture the furthest thoughts, unveiled worlds millennia away.

The audience sat in awe. The air was warm, as warm as April, though November winds blew outside.

A Sabbath Afternoon

It was a Sabbath afternoon in the year 1534.

Summertime.

The only furniture left in the dining room was a covered table. Near the table stood a coffer of books and an iron-hooped chest containing provisions for a journey—dry biscuits, smoked meats. It was obvious that the inhabitants of the house were planning a long journey.

Preparations were under way.

Master Meyer of Tannhausen was a scholar and a cabalist, one of the "great men and sages of Ashkenaz," to whom the Divine Presence had manifested itself—"he hath heard the voice of the Shechinah"—proclaiming that the Messiah, Solomon Molko, would soon bring redemption to Israel. Master Meyer had sold everything he owned in Tannhausen—his house, furniture, the courtyard with the fruit trees. He and his family were ready to set forth on the journey via Posen to Safed, whence the redemption was to come.

At the table Master Meyer was studying with his twelve-year-old son, Leibel. They were poring over the *Kaf Haketores*, a commentary on the

Book of Psalms by the cabalist Rabbi Gerson Ha-
levi, which proved that each and every verse of
Psalms proclaims redemption to be at hand. The
hundred and fifty chapters of Psalms were one long
paean to the "end of days." Employing the power
hidden in the words of the holy volume, every
pious, true Jew could destroy the enemies of Jewry.

Supposedly, the father was teaching his son.
But actually, Leibel, who at twelve was already
deeply versed in the Talmud and its commentaries,
kept interrupting his father. He asked:

"I can't understand, Father. The birth pangs
of the redemption were supposed to have begun in
the year 1492, according to the cabalistic interpretation of the seventh verse of the thirty-eighth chapter of the Book of Job. They were to have ended in
1531. But here it is already 1534. We have suffered
sufficiently from persecutions and deportations, and
yet the redemption has still not come. When *will* it
come, Father?"

"Have faith, my son, have faith." His father
grimaced, as though about to shout at his darling
Leibel. But he restrained himself, and added in a
low voice: "Though He tarry, wait for Him."

"We have no more strength to wait," Master
Meyer's wife, Hannah, cried out. "Leibel is right."

Master Meyer did not reply. He rose from the
table, and began to pace the room, in time to a tune
he hummed between clenched teeth, as an expedient
for avoiding anger. When a man grows angry he
loses his equanimity. And here Hannah too was at-
tacking him. Suddenly, he stopped pacing, as
though struck by a thought, and said to his wife:

"If you have lost your faith, Hannah, what good is the journey?"

"If the Germans were not driving us out, I should remain here." Lifting a crying baby in her arms, Hannah seated herself at the open window, where she could watch the river Main roll by, flecked with gold and silver.

"Not I." Master Meyer grasped the door knob and announced: "It is time for the Afternoon Prayer."

He left the house.

His wife looked after him with a sigh. Between the folds of her silk dress a small, bright breast, made rosy by her infant's fingers, was visible. No one would have believed that thirty-five-year-old Hannah was the mother of nine sons. At eighteen, her eldest son, Elikum Getz, the son-in-law of a Posen householder, was the head of a yeshiva in Posen. And her little Leib was the pride of all Bavaria. It was Hannah herself who had persuaded her husband to sell the house, the courtyard with the fruit trees, and to set forth on the journey. Like her husband, she too had but one longing—Safed. In Safed they would meet the redemption. But all at once—probably it was the will of God that the "birth pangs of redemption" were to be prolonged, that "Israel" was to remain on the stool of travail— Molko had been burned alive, and now the Jews were being driven out of Bavaria. And her Meyer? Meyer refused to believe that Molko had perished. He still longed for Safed. One thing she had managed to accomplish: her husband had agreed to travel by way of Posen. She was certain that her brothers, presidents of the Posen congregation, together with her son Elikum Getz, would detain Meyer in Posen, where a position awaited him, if not that of judge, then of the head of a yeshiva.

Suckling the child, Hannah rocked back and forth. She looked out the open window at the gently flowing waters of the river Main. The movement of the water was like Hannah's life here in Tannhausen, whither she had come from Posen; she felt homesick for the Warta River.

She returned the child to its crib, buttoned her dress, picked up her manuscript copy of Psalms, and sat at the window again. Her heart filled with delight as she regarded Leibel's narrow, child's shoulders and bright face. She said:

"Still, Leibel, you must not talk back to your father."

"That was not talking back, Mama." Keeping his eyes fixed on the book, the lad replied with a laugh. "And you are the one who always talks back to him, Mama."

"A wife may, but a son must respect his father."

"You are right, Mama."

His mother's reprimand made Leibel begin to regret that he had interrupted his father. He settled back into his chair, picked up the *Kaf Haketores* and leafed through the manuscript, the frontispiece of which was dated 1502.

Thirty-two years old, the manuscript looked new, as though it had just been copied by a scribe. The pages had the fresh smell of newly sawed lumber. On the flyleaf Father had written: "Purchased in the year 3 of Molko."

The inscription, with its reminder that during his lifetime Solomon Molko had been regarded as a Jewish king, as the Messiah son of David, aroused the twelve-year-old genius' enthusiasm. He knew that his father had long since stopped reckoning time according to the traditional calendar dating back to the creation of the world. He now reckoned time by the years of Molko's revelation, of Molko's reign. Nor was Father the only one. The populations of entire cities were preparing to meet the Messiah. Joyfully Jews abandoned their businesses, sold their houses and possessions at half-price, and, thus unencumbered, moved to harbor cities, where they might all the more quickly be ready to take ship for the Land of Israel. Had Molko really been killed? It was incredible. People refused to believe it. Was there to be no "reformation of hearts"? Perhaps Father was right, after all, in insisting with such positiveness that Solomon Molko was still alive!

In the twelve-year-old genius, leafing through the *Kaf Haketores,* the memory of Solomon Molko sang:

Yes, yes, yes, yes. If the holy Rabbi Judah had encompassed all of the oral teachings in the Mishnah, there would have been no ancillary traditions, no Beraitot. If not for Isaac Alfasi, if not for Maimonides, Rabbi Judah ben Asher's abridgment of the Talmud, his *Turim,* would not have been been composed. And he, Leibel—no, his name was Judah ben Meyer—he, the twelve-year-old Genius of Ashkenaz, was writing a supercommentary on all the four *Turim*. He had a title in mind. The work was to be called *Vayigash Yehudah*. Yes, that was it: *Vayigash Yehudah*.

Hannah, who was reciting psalms, intoned a melancholy counterpoint to her Leibel's proud and joyous chant. She intoned:

"Happy is the man that hath not gone in the way of the wicked."

The summery late afternoon worked its magic, distributing gold and silver with such largesse that Hannah's eyelids grew heavy. The open Book of Psalms fell from her hands, was caught briefly between the silk folds of her dress, and then slipped to the floor. When she opened her eyes again and began looking for the book, it was lying on the table.

Master Meyer returned from the Afternoon Prayer with his six younger sons. As they sat at table for the concluding Third Sabbath Meal, the Sabbath twilight was filled with the sweet scent of fields and meadows; the ringing of church bells spread a mood of uneasiness.

Master Meyer was in lively spirits at the table. He told of a letter he had received which declared that Solomon Molko had been seen in Rome. He had also been encountered on the way to Safed. Now, in the twilight, with no one interrupting him, Master Meyer began enthusiastically to tell Leibel about his grandfathers and great-grandparents. Famous cities passed in review—Mayence, Vienna, Prague, Posen, Cracow. Everywhere were kinfolk, everywhere captives were ransomed, everywhere scholarly achievement and brilliance.

Eyes closed, the twelve-year-old genius saw his grandfathers and uncles, familiar to him as though they were still alive, as familiar as the difficult pages of the talmudic tractates he knew by heart. Eagerly he questioned his father:

"Moses, Uncle Israel's son, is he really only my age? And is he called 'the Polish Genius'? How far is Cracow from Posen?"

"Moses Isserles is two years older than you," Father replied. "My son, you will catch up to him in learning. He is the Polish Genius; but you are the Genius of Ashkenaz."

"You say Moses has already composed a super-commentary on the Book of Esther?"

"Well, and you are writing a supercommentary on the *Turim!*" His father pushed his chair away from the table, as though he suddenly felt cramped. "And let me pronounce a prophecy: The world will hear from the both of you—from Rabbi Moses Isserles and Rabbi Leibel Hannahles!"

Hannah's face shone with gratification; her husband had conferred the greatest honor on her in appending her name to her son's as his surname. And when the children exclaimed: "There's a star in the sky—we can light the candles now," she remained sitting at the open window, her mother's joy close to her breast, as though she wished to hold off the "good week" with its many cares as long as she could.

Almost There

In the early morning, while the town of Bezoyn was still asleep, a passenger coach stopped in the middle of the marketplace. Three odd Jews immediately sprouted around the coach, as though they had crawled out of a hole in the ground. One by one, the passengers—tired and sleepy after a night of discomfort—left the coach and set off for home through narrow streets and lanes. The last passenger, a distinguished-looking woman, asked the wagoner:

"Master, do you know of a good hostel?"

"Fishel!" the wagoner addressed one of the odd personages, "the lady is looking for a hostel."

Fishel grabbed the woman's traveling bag and motioned to her to follow him with the thumb of his right hand. As they walked, Fishel asked, without looking at his guest:

"From Plotsk?"

"Yes."

"Do you want a bed, or a separate room?"

"A room for myself."

For the first time the hosteler turned around and gave his guest a sidelong glance. From her gait,

clothing, and in particular from the black silk shawl
that covered her wig to fall over her shoulders after
the fashion of distinguished chasidic matrons, Fishel
deduced that the woman was a rich linen or glove
merchant. But what was a merchant from Plotsk
doing in a small town like Bezoyn, when all of the
local merchants bought their merchandise in
Plotsk? Casually, he remarked:

"If there's anything you are looking for in
Bezoyn, I should be glad to be of service."

"Thank you. I am looking for the rabbi of
Bezoyn. Does he live far from the hostel?"

"Not very far. I'll have you taken to him.
What business do you have with the rabbi of
Bezoyn?"

"I need him as my arbiter. I have a suit coming
up, against my partners. It concerns a mill and a
forest, and I have been told that the rabbi of Bezoyn
is a clever man."

"Our Rabbi Meyer?" Fishel shook his head.
"people come to him for advice from all over
Poland. Rabbi Meyer has a brilliant head on him.
Where is your forest?"

"Roshchov."

"Are you one of the Bliashes?" Fishel stood
stock still, his eyes popping as though told he had
just won a fortune.

The woman smiled slightly, a smile acknowl-
edging that Fishel the hosteler had guessed cor-
rectly, she was indeed a Bliash, the wife of Leizer
Bliash, the late Leizer Bliash, to be exact—her husband had died a year and a half ago. Now Leizer's

partners were anxious to be rid of her. They wished
to buy her out, but Chaye Bliash would have none
of it. She was going to sue her partners. And that
was why she had come to Bezoyn, to ask Rabbi
Meyer to be her arbiter.

At ten o'clock that morning Chaye entered the
rabbi's house. The sexton asked her:

"What is it, a question having to do with
kosher food?"

"No, a case for arbitration."

The sexton opened the door of the courtroom.
She could enter. Chaye Bliash loosened the shawl
tied under her chin and remained standing in the
courtroom door.

"Good morning, Rabbi of Bezoyn."

"Come in, come in." The rabbi stood up behind his table, which was strewn with holy volumes,
some of which were open, some shut. Pushing a
chair forward, he returned to his seat behind the
table. "Sit down," he pointed to the chair.

The rabbi was tall and lean. The two points of
his gray-flecked black beard reached down to the
sash around his waist. The melancholy eyes were
clever.

Rabbi Meyer of Bezoyn had become a
widower at the age of forty-five. When the thirty
days of mourning were over, people began propos-
ing matches to him. Renowned for learning and
wisdom, Rabbi Meyer's clever remarks were much
quoted. Listening with half an ear, he was wont to
give all such proposals the following reply:

"God has granted me two sons. These are my

two Holy Arks. It was my late wife of blessed memory who bore me these two sons. In memory of her soul, I am studying the Mishnah—for, at bottom, there are the same consonants in the word *neshamah,* soul, as there are in the word Mishnah. I shall consent to a match when my sons have stopped reciting the Mourner's Kaddish after their mother."

All of Plotsk province repeated this reply. As a result, more people than ever before came to Bezoyn from far and wide for the rabbi's help in the most intricate suits. Rich timber merchants sent coaches for Rabbi Meyer, who unknotted and unravelled every tangled problem.

In this fashion, six months passed from the time of the death of the rabbi's wife.

The rabbi struggled. His eldest daughter, she whose husband was the town justice, attended to the needs of his household. But since she had her own household to take care of as well, there were not enough hours in the day; and when rich timber merchants came riding up to see the rabbi on business, there was no one to offer refreshments. Now, this morning, Fishel the hosteler had turned up with the message that a rich widow, the wife of the late Leizer Bliash of the Roshchover estates, had come to Bezoyn and was asking for Rabbi Meyer's help as an arbiter. The news brought a light to his eyes. Leizer, of blessed memory, had been one of the most devout Chasidim of the court of Ger, and had appointed none but learned Chasidim to manage his forests and mills. Ger had honored Leizer Bliash with a funeral oration such as was reserved for "princes in Israel." And his wife, Chaye, was spoken of as a saintly woman. Her charities were endless. Had it not been for her, the Makawe yeshiva could not have continued. That was the saintly woman who wished the rabbi of Bezoyn to be her arbiter.

Rabbi Meyer laid his colored kerchief on the open copy of the *Choshen Mishpat* that lay before him, then set the holy volume aside. Half-closing his clever eyes, he wrinkled his large, white forehead, and with the same attention he devoted to a difficult Talmudic passage listened to Chaye.

She talked about estates, mills, forests. Her Leizer had invested fifty thousand rubles here, another fifty thousand rubles there and over one hundred thousand in the estate. The enormous sums fell from Chaye's graceful lips with a pleasant ring—it was as though she were counting a string of pearls, not a list of humdrum numbers. "This is how things stand, Rabbi of Bezoyn—my partners, the Priveses and the Engelmanns, wish to buy me out, wish to buy out my share at half its value. So I am bringing a suit, Rabbi of Bezoyn, and I wish you to be my arbiter."

"You have a sure case, Madame Bliash." The rabbi made a sweeping gesture with his long fingers, riffling the pages of the *Choshen Mishpat,* as though searching for the appropriate law. "A sure case. They cannot eject you from the partnership."

The black silk shawl hanging from Chaye's head framed her face, emphasizing the pallor of her cheeks. Chaye's black, modest eyes lit up; the nobility so often encountered in the daughters of rabbis suffused her face. She laid a small hand on the table. Transparent white, the fingers were adorned with diamonds. She seemed to be struggling to speak. When she did not, the rabbi raised his eyes to hers in surprise. He was encouraged by what he saw. Lowering her eyes, Chaye said:

"I hope you will excuse my taking your time, Rabbi of Bezoyn. I wish to ask you for a piece of advice."

"What may it be?" The rabbi cupped his hand over his ear, and his clever eyes grew uneasy. "Well?"

Chaye's head inclined toward the rabbi, uncovering a clear, graceful neck. Her voice grew softer and lower:

"I have been a widow for a year and a half now. So long as my Yossel was at home, the house was full of learning, from early morning till late at night. But then he married and went off to live with his father-in-law in Lublin. And now the bookcases have become widows, as I am. No one opens them any more. There are the holy tractates of the Talmud in my home, and other holy volumes, but there is no one to open them, no one to study them. The melody of Torah, the melody of Talmud, has vanished from my home. May God be punishing me? After all, I am nothing but a sinful woman. . . ."

"The best thing to do is to remarry," the rabbi murmured.

"That is what I think, Rabbi of Bezoyn."

There was a moment of silence. The rabbi's ear remained cupped, as he waited for Chaye to come to the point—the point he had himself made.

All at once he rose from the table, growing taller. He took a volume of the Talmud from an upper shelf of his bookcase, and began leafing through it as he stood. Then, closing the volume, he brightened and said, as though speaking to himself.

"Almost there, almost there. . . ."

Chaye did not raise her eyes. Her white fingers strayed along the dark fringes of her shawl. Now she spoke in a still quieter voice, as though confiding a secret:

"Before journeying to you, Rabbi of Bezoyn, I visited at Ger, to lament that the Torah had departed from my home. The rabbi said to me: 'Rabbi Meyer of Bezoyn has been widowed.' "

"Indeed?" Stooping somewhat, the rabbi stood in the middle of the courtroom. As he listened to Chaye speak, everything about him flamed up— eyes, beard, lips; the point had been reached, the point he himself had suggested.

Ben Sira's Grandson

When Eleazar ben Jeshua, the cantor and scribe of the Great Synagogue of Alexandria, stepped out of his home that afternoon, the Delta—the crowded Jewish quarter—was impassable.

On every hand merchants, from China, India, Persia, Syria, Rome, were hurrying to shops and factories where cotton, rugs, brocades were woven, glass blown, perfume distilled.

Freight wagons piled one and two stories high, some drawn by horses, others by men, rattled through the broad avenues toward the harbor, where ships waited at anchor to bear the merchandise to China, India, Persia, Syria, and Rome.

Eleazar ben Jeshua was a tall man with a slight stoop. His loose black cloak was buttoned up to the neck. His hands were clasped behind him; the ends of scrolls, some of paper, others of very thin parchment, stuck out from his deep pockets.

He cut across the long side of the Delta triangle, an occasional smile brightening his spade-bearded, long, overcast face, as he returned the salute of factory owners, merchants, artisans, and common folk making way for their cantor and scribe to pass.

The owner of a perfumery, a short personage with broad shoulders, emerged. In one hand he held garlands of saffron, in the other strings of pepper. The perfume merchant stopped Eleazar:

"Good day, cantor of Alexandria. Could you tell me when the holiday falls this year on the isle of Pharos?"

"The same as every year, Levitas—on the eighth day of Tebet."

A crowd developed as one person after another lent an ear to the conversation. A circle formed around the cantor. One curious person inquired:

"Is it really true that the King and Queen have promised to attend the ceremonies?"

"Yes, it is true." The cantor smiled through his spade beard, the long face grew longer still.

"And is it really true," stuttered a shy man, "that you, Alexandrian cantor, have prepared a 'Mount Sinai' play for the new converts?"

"Indeed, and with thunder and lightning!" interjected a third man. The crowd was agape.

The cantor did not reply. Good-humoredly, he removed two Arabic peppers from the perfume merchant's string, put one in his mouth, the other in his pocket, and went on his way.

Eleazar ben Jeshua entered the Gamma quarter. Though fewer Jews resided here, Gamma had three synagogues, one where Egyptian Jews worshipped, one for Roman Jews, and one for the Macedonians, whose ancestors had helped build Alexandria. Indeed, Alexandria was truly a Jewish

city, every third inhabitant being a Jew. Of the
city's one million two hundred thousand souls, some
four hundred thousand were Jewish. That is not to
say that the remaining eight hundred thousand were
Egyptian. There were people in Alexandria from all
over the world. But none of the other groups could
compare with the Jewish one, which was the largest
and richest.

Every year the Jews of Alexandria celebrated
the eighth day of Tebet, the anniversary of the
translation of the Hebrew Bible into Greek.

The Jewish garrison had already cleared the
seacoast of the isle of Pharos and begun to erect
tents. This year the most important city fathers
were expected to attend—the heads of the army, the
royal suite, with their entire families. Then there
were the converts: over one thousand pagans were
being converted to Judaism this year. Eleazar had
written a special "Mount Sinai" play for them; it
would be presented near the new lighthouse.

But the solemnity of the occasion, and the
holiday as a whole, meant very little to the Alexandrian scribe at that moment. He knew that the
presentation of the "Mount Sinai" play was merely
a diversion. What was essential was the reading in
Greek of extracts from the holy Five Books of
Moses and the Prophets. Other books, not yet
canonized as part of the Bible, would be read as
well. And if Theodorus could read extracts from the
Scroll of Esther, why should not Eleazar ben
Jeshua read from his grandfather's *Proverbs of Ben*

Sira? How could you compare *Esther* with *Ben Sira?* There was no comparison!

Suddenly there was a bitter taste in Eleazar ben Jeshua's mouth. His sharp white teeth had just bitten into the Arabic pepper he had been sucking.

As for him, he knew who the author of the *Scroll of Esther* was—a disciple of Simeon ben Sira, Eleazar's grandfather. The author would never have received the appellation of "sage and scribe" were it not for Grandfather. Yet here, wherever one went, it was *Scroll of Esther* this, *Scroll of Esther* that—as though it were about the Jews of Alexandria, and not those of Persia. The local anti-Semites, people insisted, were the same as the Persian Haman, not one whit different.

Eleazar ben Jeshua entered the large city park. He passed the museum, the mausoleum where Alexander of Macedonia lay embalmed in a crystal coffin. Eleazar turned right, and went up stone steps that led to the library. Hundreds of marble columns graced the entrance, where flocks of doves nested. On either side of the entry were fountains at whose alabaster mouths the thirsty could drink.

The library was crowded. Over five hundred librarians moved softly in felt sandals, fetching readers paper and parchment scrolls in small, narrow reed baskets.

For years Eleazar ben Jeshua had been hard at work on his grandfather's *Proverbs of Ben Sira,* which he was translating into Greek, but he was still dissatisfied. One of the chief Pharisees of Alex-

andria, he could not agree with his grandfather's
views on reward and punishment. He was mostly
troubled over the fact that his grandfather denied
the doctrine of resurrection. Eleazar never spoke of
this matter to strangers. But in the privacy of his
own heart, he was forced to admit it. Nor was
Grandfather the only skeptic! It was with this problem that Eleazar ben Jeshua had come to visit
Antigonus, one of the chief librarians of Alexandria, and a boyhood friend from their student
days in Jerusalem.

At Eleazar's greeting, short Antigonus raised a
pair of lively blue eyes from the parchments unrolled before him. The comrades regarded one another in joyful silence for a moment. Then they fell
to talking, half in Greek, half in Aramaic. Eleazar
placed two scrolls on the table. His comrade asked
in a low voice:

"Have you amended the verse about resurrection?"

"No, I have not amended it," Eleazar said
slowly. "What I have done is to reinterpret it according to the tradition."

"One need do no more."

Eleazar ben Jeshua unrolled one of the scrolls,
which was in Hebrew, then the other, the Greek
translation. These were two copies of the *Proverbs
of Ben Sira*.

The comrades bent over the parchments.
The joy fled from their eyes. Their faces clouded,
foreheads wrinkled with concentration.

The Hebrew text read:

"Lower thy pride greatly, greatly,
For man's hope is but deceitful."

In the Greek it had become:

"Lower thy spirit to the earth,
For the punishment of the nonbeliever is fire
and worms."

Both men raised their shoulders, raised their heads. They were equally delighted at the interpretation. Eleazar thrust his hand into his deep pocket, found the Arabic pepper, and offered it to his comrade. It disappeared behind Antigonus' fleshy lips. There was joy in their eyes, joy in their beards. And when Antigonus, drawing his comrade toward him, said in a very, very low voice, almost whispering in his ear, "The Hebrew text has to be altered too, or the Pharisees will find further reason to complain," Eleazar did not reply.

He had been thinking the same thought for a long time. But each time he sat down over the Hebrew scroll with the intention of altering it, he could not lift his hands to the task. Eleazar felt guilty toward his grandfather. After all, he had inserted another meaning into Grandfather's text, another sense. This was something he had to confide to Antigonus.

But Eleazar suddenly found himself standing alone. Behind the bust of Socrates, Antigonus was ringed about by a group of young people, to whom he was explaining the genesis of language according to Plato's dialogue *Cratylus.*

Eleazar rolled up the scrolls, placed them in his deep pockets, and considered whether to bid Antigonus farewell. Deciding not to disturb the librarian, he made for the exit. The path between the marble pillars was now impassable. Dozens, hundreds of doves flew about, cooing. Eleazar halted. He looked at the flaming red sun setting in the slimy Nile, and was seized with sadness. He thought to himself:

"If I have inserted another meaning in your writing, Grandfather, forgive me. When books like *Job,* and the *Song of Songs,* and the *Scroll of Esther* become part of the holy canon, let not your *Proverbs of Ben Sira* be omitted. I have done what I did, Grandfather, not for my own sake, but out of reverence for you. Forgive me, Grandfather."

Father, Father

Miss Lazarus, a history teacher in New York City's Morris High School, went twice a week to Park Avenue near 160th Street in the Bronx where Dinah Granat lived. Dinah was a student of Miss Lazarus' who had been bedridden for months with a bad heart.

Miss Lazarus was unhappy. She had promised Dinah to be there at about four o'clock, and it was already five. She hurried, although the narrow sidewalk on Park Avenue was frozen and slippery, and one might easily fall and hurt oneself. As she rushed, the strands of gray hair slipped out from her fur hat, contrasting with her youthful face, pinched with the cold.

She arrived in front of the apartment house where Dinah lived—an old, faded building, where dark letter boxes, from which the nameplates had been torn, grimaced like toothless mouths. The streaked windows looked out on an iron fence. Behind the fence lay tracks over which trains clattered noisily every half hour. For a long time after a train had disappeared down the tracks, the distant reverberation of its wheels pulsated in the three small rooms of Dinah's apartment, like the humming of telegraph wires.

Until sometime after noon, the invalid was almost always alone at home. Her father had a pushcart on Bathgate Avenue where he sold tailor's remnants. Her two little brothers played outdoors, and sixteen-year-old Dinah lay in bed, alone in the house.

It was not until three or four in the afternoon that people began to appear. Then, different teachers arrived, volunteers who were helping Dinah get through her high school courses. Afterward came her boy friends and girl friends, comrades from the Kevutzah camp which Dinah had attended the past three summers. Together they had learned to cultivate the soil, milk cows, look after a farm. The young comrades behaved like members of a religious sect. Entering Dinah's room softly, on tiptoe, they offered their sick comrade a quiet, warm Shalom. They came in groups, five or six at a time, to stand around Dinah's bed with joy in their eyes, youth and vigor in every limb.

In the early evening they all studied Hebrew together, speaking low, their voices trembling, as though it was not a foreign language they were studying but some secret teaching. Later, they sang songs, sitting on the floor near Dinah's bed; singing softly, they dreamed that the war would end soon and they would be able to cross the sea to join a collective settlement in Palestine.

Dinah, a tall girl with long arms and legs, had matured during the six months she lay in bed, as a winter apple ripens prematurely in a heated room. She had grown prettier, and did not look sick at all—certainly not mortally sick. Her face had filled out, her complexion had become clear and bright, and the dark blond hair in two thick braids which came down over the blanket was charming. But her eyes, shy, introspective, alternately blue or green, were always feverish. When she engaged in conversation, it was hard to tell the cause of the fever—whether it was her sick heart, or her constant worry. For Dinah always had something to worry about. Either she was suffering out of sympathy for the Jews in the concentration camps and ghettos, suffering because she was not there with them, or else she was suffering because England had closed the doors of Palestine to Jewish immigrants. All the time she lay in bed she grieved because she could no longer persuade boys or girls to join the Zionist movement, because she would not be able to go to the Zionist camp this year. Yet there was also an element of joy in her worry. Dinah was proud of the Jewish uprising in the Warsaw Ghetto, very proud indeed of Comrade Tosha, who had fought the foe in the Warsaw Ghetto and fallen. Dinah had not known Tosha personally. But, finding Tosha's picture in a newspaper, she had cut it out and hung it over her bed; there it shone, glowed, a face suffused with love of life and humanity.

Dinah spoke passionately about almost all subjects, her green eyes blazing—about everything, that is, except her own sickness and the grinding poverty in her own home.

Once when Dinah, in a fit of particular anxiety, left her bed, her father, a fervent Chasid, took his daughter in his arms and brought her back to bed. He implored:

"Darling, the doctor told you never to get out of bed, for the love of God. Are you trying to harm yourself?"

Dinah grew angry at her father:

"The Jewish people is sicker than I am, and what are you doing about it?"

If Adam Granat had not been ashamed of such a gesture, he would have kissed his daughter for that remark. Unable to speak, he moved about Dinah's room, humming to himself a melody which revealed that it did indeed matter to him that the Jewish people was sick, it mattered very much, but what could he, a poor Jewish peddler, do about it?

Later, he went into the deserted kitchen. There he said out loud, as though talking to his wife, delighted finally to be able to speak:

"You should have heard what your daughter just said to me, Esther. . . . A deep saying, Esther . . . a deep saying."

It no longer mattered to him that his legs trembled as he sat at table or stood at work. It no longer mattered to him that the three iron beds, piled high with spreads, pillows, and cushions, were in disarray. Nor did it matter that in the small rooms which the kitchen oven could never warm sufficiently the air was damp, smelling of the wet wash always drying on ropes stretched from wall to wall.

The six-foot man paced back and forth through the kitchen, repeating his daughter's remark:

"The Jewish people is sicker than I am, and what are you doing about it, Father?"

Did it really matter to him?

Oh, but it did matter, it did matter!

In exactly the same fashion, he used to spend hours during his youth in the prayer room at Kotsk, pacing all afternoon long as he tried to fathom what Rabbi Mendele had intended by his interpretation of the first words of Moses' farewell address to the Jewish people: "*Haazinu hashomayim,* Hearken, O heavens." Rabbi Mendele had interpreted the words as meaning: "Hearken in a heavenly fashion."

What did "in a heavenly fashion" mean? Indeed, what did it mean? What did "the Jewish people is sick" mean. Yes, it is sick. But what could he, a six-foot man, do? Beat his head against the wall? If that would help, he would beat his head against the wall....

It was five o'clock, and the unheated rooms were dark. The sound of Dinah's father groaning could be heard as he paced the kitchen. He had just come in from the street.

What was he groaning about?

Because there was no coal in the coal bucket? Because the fire in the iron stove was about to go out? No—he was flushed with agitation, and did not feel the cold. He was suffering because Dinah had accidentally burned one of her toes.

Dinah's father stopped pacing, and listened at the closed door.

"Someone coming?"

Miss Lazarus walked up the narrow, dark steps. At every landing, her throat and nose were assailed by cooking smells. When she finally reached Dinah's flight, it was so dark that the teacher was uncertain whether she was standing at the right door until she put out her hand and touched the mezuzah on the doorpost.

"This is where Dinah lives."

A descendant of an old Sephardic Jewish family, Miss Lazarus had fallen so deeply in love with Dinah and her parents that she had become a student of Hebrew. She studied Hebrew with Dinah, spent her summers in the Kevutzah camp, and dreamed of living and working in a collective settlement in Palestine.

Miss Lazarus opened the door and called out in a Boston accent:

"Hello there, Dinah! Sorry to be late, dear."

Dinah's father, broad-shouldered and tall, blocked Miss Lazarus' way.

"What a misfortune!"

"Why, is something wrong? Has anything happened?" Miss Lazarus removed her hat, unexpectedly revealing light gray tresses above her youthful, girlish face.

"Sick heart and all," Dinah's father pointed to the room where Dinah lay, "she has burned her toe."

"Oh no!" The teacher winced, as though it were she who had burned her toe and not Dinah.

Each time she had occasion to talk to Dinah's father, Miss Lazarus gazed with astonishment at this lanky man with the blue, childish eyes. The sparse, brown beard was graying. And the soft black hat he wore pushed back to the nape of his neck, and the pale, broad, deeply wrinkled forehead were more appropriate to a university professor than to a Bathgate Avenue peddler. He took Miss Lazarus by the hand and spoke in low tones:

"You know, teacher, it is better never to have been born than to be poor. All these years I have been in America, I still haven't been able to afford a hot water bottle. She was cold, the poor child's feet were cold, she couldn't warm up. How could she be warm with a hole in her heart? So, I took a hot pan from the stove, wrapped it in a handkerchief, and placed it near her feet. I don't know what happened —the handkerchief must have become loose—but Dinah burned her little toe. It is a bad burn—I burned my daughter myself." His blue eyes flashed with anxiety and self-reproach. "A fine father I am! Do you understand what I mean, Miss Lazarus?" He stooped down to the short teacher. "The child is sick, desperately sick, and it's such a humiliation. . . . Do you see how big I am? A man over six feet tall, a father who can't buy his sick daughter a little thing like a hot water bag."

Miss Lazarus had enormous respect for Dinah's father. She had never met a Jew of this type; all her relations were successful middle-class people

—doctors with reputation, eminent lawyers, well-to-do business men. The sight of Dinah's father poring over a sacred volume and humming as he studied, reminded her of the patriarchs of old, or of the pious Jews who had fled Spain. And now this noble man was standing before her, bemoaning his lot. There must be some way of helping such a man— he *must* be helped in order to save Dinah's life. As Miss Lazarus stood thus, lost in thought, she heard Dinah's voice:

"Don't you listen to him, Miss Lazarus. It's just a burned toe, but to my father it's a tragedy!"

"Hear her, teacher!" The father's face lit up. "Dinah will never complain about herself. If she were to complain, just once, I'd pawn the shirt off my back—she could have anything she wants from me. But she refuses to complain, she accepts everything as being for the best!"

Two small boys appeared at the open door, one nine years old, the other seven. Both were sweaty, tearful, frightened, neglected, shabby. The younger boy pointed to his brother:

"Papa, Hershel broke a window!"

"Where?" asked his father.

"I did not!" Pulling his cap down over his eyes, the older boy sidled away from his father.

The janitress, hatless, her coat unbuttoned, swept into the room without a word, as though into her own home.

Mr. Granat was two months behind in the rent; meekly he came over to the janitress, a smile twisting his lips.

"I know all about it, I know. But what am I to do?" He put out both hands to the janitress. "Shall I flog the skin off the rascal's back? His sister is sick, deathly sick, and this little hoodlum runs around breaking windows!"

The janitress stationed herself in the middle of the kitchen, arms akimbo.

"It wouldn't hurt for you to teach the boy a lesson. Give him a good beating. . . . But first off, send for a glazier and have a new pane put in today. It's winter—make it right away!"

Miss Lazarus was about to offer to go for the glazier when Dinah's father suddenly leaped at the janitress.

"What do you want from us?" He grabbed her arms and began to skake her back and forth. "For two months rent, for a new window-pane you want me to skin Hershel alive? Is that all? Isn't there anything else you want? There's a bread knife on the table—it's dull but it will do!" Lowering his head, Adam stretched out his neck, like an ox, for the slaughter. "Slaughter me too while you are at it. Go ahead—slaughter me!"

Miss Lazarus intervened. She escorted the janitress to the door; terrified, her face bloodless, the janitress could be heard repeating time and again on the other side of the door:

"Crazy man! Crazy man!"

Dinah called to her father:

"Papa, if you don't stop yelling, I'll come out of bed barefoot!"

His eyes and hands pleading, Adam begged

Miss Lazarus to go to Dinah. Left alone in the kitchen, he paced back and forth for some time. Then he leaned one hand on a kitchen wall, laid his head on his hand, and murmured softly:

"Father, Father. . . . One cries and cries to Father for help, until he becomes a father. . . . Father, Father. . . ."

In a Slaughterhouse

The city was still asleep when Meyer the butcher came riding into town with a wagonload of calves for Samuel David the slaughterer. Sitting among the calves were the butcher's four sons. They kept their eyes fixed on the three-year-old bull, which was bound to the wagon by a chain. The wagon had barely stopped when one of the boys was knocking at the slaughterer's window:

"Master Samuel David, are you sleeping there? Don't forget your big knife, Master Samuel David!"

Some time passed before the slaughterer came out of the tumbledown hut, his smock flying. He was a tall, thin man, with a sparse beard and red eyes. In one hand he held a big, wooden slaughterer's sheath; with the other, he straightened out his prayer vest and began to button his coat.

Meyer the butcher gave the slaughterer a hand and silently gestured to him to clamber into the wagon using a wheel as ladder. When the wagon moved, the slaughterer was sitting among the calves, his face to the bull.

The horses pulled hard. The bull tugged back.

The chain attached to the iron ring in the bull's nose stretched to its full length.

The bull roared; the cows mooed sadly, breaking the early morning silence.

The slaughterer avoided the bull's blood-filled, murderous eyes. He sat trembling, as though he had not been a slaughterer for more than thirty years, as though this were his first experience in slaughtering a bull. And he had cause to tremble. One could never be certain with a bull as dangerous as this one. Samuel David had killed more than one bull badly, making it non-kosher. Once Moshe had beaten him so badly for just such a failure with the "sin-offering" that Samuel David had kept to his bed for weeks afterward.

The horses turned off to the road leading to the slaughterhouse. Bending his head and rearing his back, the bull ran after the wagon with a violence presaging an attack on the slaughterer. Suddenly, the bull smelled blood and roared so loudly that the early morning air trembled. Homeless dogs began to bark. The lads from the slaughterhouse came running up, threw the calves over their shoulders, and dragged them off into the slaughterhouse.

Meyer the butcher and his sons busied themselves with the bull. They tied a wet rag around his eyes, then skillfully threw a rope around three of his legs. When they had dragged him into the slaughterhouse, they tugged and the bull fell hard on the lime floor; the brick wall shook. Every available man in the slaughterhouse hurled himself at the bull; they sat on his bound legs and bristly back and hung on to his horns. While the skinner began shaving the bull's neck with a razor, Meyer the butcher went over to the slaughterer, who was checking his blade at an oil lamp. The butcher bent down:

"Master Samuel David. . . ."

The slaughterer did not reply. He stood rigid, as though possessed. The butcher's voice trembled:

"If, God forbid, this bull becomes non-kosher, I'll be left with nothing but my whip . . . Master Samuel David, do you hear?"

Samuel David sighed.

The bright oil lamp hanging in the slaughterhouse dazzled the slaughterer's eyes; he could not see for a moment. Rubbing his eyes, he caught sight of the dangerous bull, surrounded by so many faces and so many hands. The next moment he was sitting on the bull's back with the boys. The bull glowered at him, thrusting a pair of wild, bloody eyes into Samuel David's face.

His hands did not tremble. Firmly he held the knife, in whose broad blade the slaughterhouse boys, the bull, and the slaughterer were all mirrored. His lips murmured the benediction. He cut badly, missing the obligatory "signs." Blood spurted. Voices:

"He has finished off the bull!"

"The pox take him!"

"What, not kosher?" Meyer the butcher grabbed the slaughterer by the lapels. "Not kosher?"

"Who says so?" The slaughterer was half-dead with fright.

"Well, is it kosher?"

"Of course . . . certainly it is kosher."

It was five o'clock in the morning. The slaughterhouse path was still empty. Master Motke, the fowl slaughterer, had still not arrived. The early morning air was filled with the cackling of chickens and the barking of dogs. Samuel David wiped his sweaty forehead, unable to recover, not believing his eyes. The rabbi was approaching the slaughterhouse. He would have to deal with the rabbi—a strict man, a rigorist. Today, of all days, he wished to examine the slaughterer's blade.

In terror the slaughterer left the slaughterhouse through an open window. He considered running away to the fields. Instead, he got down on all fours next to the wall, and saw a homeless dog. He was amazed that the dog did not run away from him in terror.

Voices from the slaughterhouse. Meyer the butcher and his sons were clamoring:

"Where is the slaughterer? He was here a second ago!"

The rabbi did not shout, but his warning was loud:

"Let it be known to you, Meyer, that this bull is not kosher. Let it also be known to you that henceforth it is forbidden to eat anything slaughtered by Samuel David. I consider him a slaughterer no longer. As for you Meyer, be most careful: the day you sell this bull as kosher, that same day at prayers I shall inform the entire congregation that you are a deliberate sinner."

The tall, thin slaughterer broke away from the wall. His mind was clouded. On his bent shoulders lay two score years spent here, in the slaughterhouse. At home—a wife and seven children. Now, all at once—no more slaughterhouse, no more slaughterer. A homeless dog. The blood pounded in his temples. There was confusion in his mind. He pulled himself up through the window, ran back into the slaughterhouse and shouted, as though possessed:

"What, the bull is not kosher? I, Samuel David the slaughterer, am kosher!"

And, with a single flourish of his knife, he cut his throat from ear to ear and fell on the limestone floor.

Butchers, flayers, helpers—all ran to the slaughterer.

Meyer, the butcher, was the first to shout:

"Where is that rabbi, the murderer?"

"Yes, where is he?" voices echoed.

"He was frightened and left."

"What we ought to do," Meyer the butcher stormed, "is lay the corpse in the rabbi's courtroom."

"Don't do it, Meyer," begged an old butcher.

No one paid the old man any heed.

Meyer and his sons seized the body of the slaughterer, which was still warm, and placed it in the wagon. Meyer picked up the reins, the wagon moved, and the slaughterhouse crew jumped in. As they neared the city, people appeared:

"What is it?"

"Who has died?"

Meyer rushed the corpse into the rabbi's courtroom. The rabbi, wearing his prayer shawl for morning prayers, was putting on the arm phylacteries; he moved off toward the window at the unexpected intrusion. Shoving aside the table strewn with holy volumes, the butcher ordered the corpse laid on the floor. It stared triumphantly at the rabbi. The rabbi stood paralyzed, as though he had lost the power to speak. Only his pale, bare arms with the unwrapped leather thongs of the phylacteries trembled.

Midnight Vigil

It was a rainy night after the High Holy Days, the kind of dark autumn night one finds only in small Polish towns where the darkness seems to be raining black ink before one's eyes.

On such a night, "big-boned" Simcha the wagoner turned restlessly in bed, unable to fall asleep. The large room with the alcove and kitchen was completely dark. The warm air was heavy with smells: ground coffee, prunes, almonds, and dates. Snoring resounded from the alcove where Simcha's two sons, Wolf and Fishel, were sleeping.

The railroad line from Warsaw to Berlin had just been completed. Wolka, two *versts* from Mlawa, was on the Russian-German border. With the coming of the railroad, Mlawa revived, as wagoners transported goods from the freight yard to the city. And the most successful of all the wagoners was "big-boned" Simcha. He, his two sons, and his "help," Velvel, all four drove freight wagons loaded with merchandise, from which they took a "cut"— not Simcha so much as his sons. The "cut"—sacks of almonds, coffee, prunes—was stored in Simcha's home. His fortune increased. He built himself a house with a granary and stable for his three huge horses. Simcha's sons, the terror of the freight yard, allowed no one to stand in their way.

In those prosperous days, when the whole city envied Simcha his good fortune, his best horse, the white one with the white stocking feet, collapsed—not while working, but in the stable, as though he had been poisoned. While Simcha was still dickering over a replacement, his three-year-old Bulan collapsed in the stable as well.

Now Simcha was sure that both horses had been poisoned; every wagoner at the freight yard was his enemy. All because of his sons, who were always fighting. Standing over the fallen horse with his sons and Velvel, Simcha said:

"Listen boys. If they keep poisoning a horse a week, we'll have nothing left but whips. Until I catch the one who did it red-handed, I have to keep quiet. But, beginning today, we have to keep our eye on the horses at the freight yard. Velvel, from now on, you spend the night in the stable with the horses."

With the death of his horses, a change took place in Simcha. He was one of those men who would rather break than bend. Simcha refused to bend. He kept up appearances, buying two freight horses as replacements, and good ones, too.

But at night, turning from side to side in bed, he was sorely troubled at the thought that God had turned against him, of all people. Why? True, Simcha was a simple man. He scarcely knew the prayers and that more by rote than from the prayer book. But who donated with a more generous hand than Simcha? Never a Sabbath passed without a guest or two at his table. And when the rabbi came for a contribution, the smallest coin he ever received was a silver ruble.

Then why had God punished him?

It was past midnight, but Simcha could not fall asleep. He stared into the darkness and listened to the sound of snoring, like boards being sawed. If Simcha had been able to read the small script, he would have lit a candle and pored over a holy volume.

Sighing deeply, Simcha began to dress in the dark. The floor squeaked as he put on his boots.

"Where are you going, Simcha?" called out his wife, sleeping in a nearby bed.

"I can't stay in bed, Hannah," Simcha apologized. "I'm going out to have a look at the horses."

"You don't think I've been able to shut an eye!"

Simcha did not reply. He pulled the belt more tightly around his trousers, took his whip, and went out into the courtyard. A chill rain was dripping down. The sky was dark. Simcha entered the stable where an oil lamp was smoking. The horses raised their heads at their master's entrance. Simcha stroked all three in turn. Velvel turned over on his bed of hay.

"Who's there?"

"It's me, Velvel. Go back to sleep!"

Simcha left the stable. He counted the freight wagons with his whip: one, two, three. But he would only be able to harness two wagons. Disconsolately, he spat, cracked the whip, and went out into the street. The wet darkness leaned against Simcha like a wall. He stood for a while, eyes shut, listening to the rain dully falling; he thought he heard a strangled weeping. He left Potter Street and set out toward the marketplace. The weeping grew more distinct. A small flame cut through the darkness. Where was the light? At the rabbi's?

Simcha stood before the house where the rabbi lived. From the courtroom, where a flame flickered in the window, came a low weeping. Who was that crying? The rabbi's wife? Was a child sick? Perhaps they needed help. Whip in hand, Simcha ascended the dark steps. It was not until he stood before the courtroom door that Simcha perceived that it was the rabbi who was weeping. A tremor ran through his body—the rabbi was weeping. Half of Poland prided itself on Rabbi Wolf Lipschitz. The elder brother was Rabbi Moshe of Lodz, the younger was Rabbi Wolf of Mlawa, and the sister, Prive, was the wife of the rabbi of Kutno.

Simcha opened the courtroom door, and was seized with terror. The rabbi of Mlawa was sitting on the floor. In one hand he held a candle, in the other a holy volume, and he was chanting a melancholy singsong.

"What is wrong, Rabbi of Mlawa?" The wagoner raised his whip. "Is the Rabbi of Mlawa sitting for the Seven Days of Mourning? Who has died?"

"No, Simcha," the rabbi calmed the wagoner. "I am observing the midnight vigil."

"What is that, the 'midnight vigil'?" Simcha gestured in ignorance.

"The Holy Temple was destroyed, the Divine Presence is in Exile," the rabbi intoned in the same melancholy singsong. "We Jews must recite the Book of Lamentations, we must cry and wail."

"Woe is me, woe is me!" Simcha grasped his head with his hands. "The Holy Temple was destroyed! Woe is me!"

The wagoner began to moan, as though he had just learned of the destruction of the Temple. He beat his fists against his head. If the rabbi of Mlawa wept, could Simcha the wagoner be silent? He would not be silent. He banged his head against the wall with such fury that his forehead began to bleed. Frightened, the rabbi sprang to his feet. He put his arms around the wagoner's shoulders, and tried to calm him down:

"Simcha, you will hurt yourself! You've made yourself all bloody. Please sit down, sit down!"

Seating the wagoner, the rabbi wiped his bloody forehead with his kerchief, and asked him several times:

"Would you like a drink of water?"

"No, Rabbi of Mlawa." The wagoner felt uncomfortable at the rabbi's attentions. "I don't want any water. But I would like some whisky. A drink of whisky would make me feel less sad at heart."

"But I have no whisky!" the rabbi cried apologetically. He began rummaging through the cupboards.

Simcha the wagoner left the courtroom and returned before long with a decanter of whisky.

232

Placing it on the table, he poured two tumblers full. "If I feel sad at heart because the Holy Temple is destroyed," he said, "you, Rabbi of Mlawa, must certainly feel even worse. So let us have some whisky."

When they had both drunk, Simcha poured again. After the third glass, the rabbi of Mlawa, feeling better, pushed the glass away and, with a learned smile in his clever eyes, said: "Enough, Simcha, enough."

"How can that be enough, Rabbi of Mlawa?" The wagoner had finished his third glass—and a fourth and a fifth as well. "How can that be enough, Rabbi of Mlawa, when we Jews are being persecuted. . . . The Holy Temple is in ruins. . . . God has put a curse on my house. . . . The last two weeks, my two best horses have died. . . . God wishes to undo me. . . . I feel bad, Rabbi of Mlawa." Simcha poured out a seventh glass. "I want to scream and cry. . . . The Holy Temple is in ruins, and Simcha the wagoner has been left with nothing but his whip —no more wealth, no more on good terms with God."

"Now, now, Simcha." The rabbi led the wagoner to the sofa in the courtroom. "How will you ever get home in this state of mind? Sleep here tonight. Ah well, lie down, lie down. . . . Good night, Simcha!" The rabbi covered him with an overcoat. "Good night!"

For a moment the rabbi stood at the door, candle in one hand, the *New Light* in the other. When Simcha turned to the wall, the rabbi left the courtroom.

Lampshade King

Silence reigned—the silence of a cathedral.

Irving Treves, alone, contemplated the deep-set, arched windows, the two marble columns, the paneled walls that absorbed all sound, repelling the din rising from Fifth Avenue and Broadway in New York City. The arched ceiling and the muted light streaming from the walls like the glow of waxed candles emphasized the shadows around the columns. Were it not for the black oak desk that occupied one entire wall, this might have been taken for a house of prayer, rather than Treves' business office.

Three maps hung on the wall—the United States, Asia and Africa, and Europe. The American map, the largest of the three, resembled a battlefield. The places where Treves' customers were located were pinned with American flags, red, white and blue. Flags dotted the states, heavily in certain areas, more sparsely in others.

Treves rose and gazed at the map of the United States, like a victorious field marshal. The profusion of flags was conclusive evidence that the war was long since won, the enemy defeated. The few competitors who had moved their factories to the hinterlands, to undercut Treves with cheap labor, were languishing.

Treves had achieved the position of the biggest manufacturer of lampshades in the United States. The small flags represented the hundreds of cities where Treves supplied merchants, where he had customers in the thousands. It was Treves who dictated prices, dictated fashions in lampshades. Broadway called him the Lampshade King. His factory in New Jersey, with two thousand hands working around the clock on day and night shifts, needed to be enlarged. This was a problem Treves did not discuss with his managers. He was a man who did not care to ask for advice. When a new project presented itself to his attention, he would first work it through in his own mind—a process that took days, sometimes weeks. Once he decided on a program, it was up to his managers to execute it faithfully. That was Treves' method of operation. In order to plan, Treves required solitude. He had sectioned off one-third of the entire floor he occupied and had it renovated. The result was a suite that was a cross between a temple and a cathedral, where every thought was converted into prayer.

Treves moved over to the second map. His gaze swept over the few flags in Asia and Africa. There were no flags at all in the third map, that of Europe. Treves was determined to gain a foothold in France. He was disturbed by the fact that the Germans had flooded the European lampshade market.

He knew that competing with Germany was

madness. German labor was dirt cheap, the cost of raw material practically zero. Driving out the Germans would mean throwing away one hundred thousand dollars, one-tenth of Treves' fortune. And afterward? When Treves set about raising prices again, what certainty would he have that the French would not go back to the Germans? This was a risky venture, it meant gambling with the devil. Treves knew that no one but a hot-headed idiot would even consider it. But he could not help himself. He was impelled, painfully impelled, to take the measure of Germany. And he had the means to put up a stake. At this point it did not matter to him that he might lose a tenth, or a third, or even half of his entire fortune. Disagreeing with the Communists, it was his position that, like the proletariat, capital was not truly international. The World War had proved that. If the capitalists of the democratic world opposed Nazi Germany, it would collapse, as Treves' opponents had collapsed. Nor did Treves put much faith in the iron laws of economics. He did not believe that overproduction necessarily caused economic crisis. There had been overproduction in the automobile market for years. Twice as many cars as were needed were being produced. Every automobile was produced for the luxury market—and *luxury* was giving employment to millions of workers. As for Nazi Germany, what about the emotional considerations—the anger and bitterness and hostility—that are always capable of upsetting so-called "economic laws"? Treves knew that he did not stand alone. There were men like him in England and France and Holland. They must think like him, too. With their backing, Treves was certain he would not only drive the Germans out of the lampshade business; he would dominate the entire French market, as he had dominated the American one.

The very thought bred a restlessness in Treves; his office all at once grew too confining. He opened a massive door and began to pace the entire seventeenth floor.

Treves moved through two rows of typewriters, past steel filing cabinets. He entered the showroom, as big as an Oriental bazaar. Dozens of burning floor lamps barely lit up the lampshades piled high on show like pyramids, cones with their apexes cut.

It was quiet. The staff had all left at five o'clock; only Treves and his chauffeur remained. The time was six. In ten minutes Treves was to be connected with Paris by telephone. Bijour, with more than one hundred shops in France, was to make his first order, for fifty thousand dollars. In filling it, Treves would lose ten thousand dollars.

Sitting among the lampshade pyramids like a carved Buddha, was a fat Korean—Treves' chauffeur. He was staring into the half-lit room, disregarding his master, his lips moving, as if in silent debate.

Treves had passed his chauffeur when he suddenly turned around. The Korean was still opening and shutting his mouth like a frog. Treves asked him: "Whom are you cursing, Chen?"

"The enemy of my country, Japan."

"Listen, Chen: How much would you pay me to drive the Japanese out of Korea?"

"All the money I have in the world, master."

The Korean rose. His face glowed, his small eyes turned into slits. He spoke rapidly, swallowing the difficult English words:

"My countrymen are holding six hundred dollars for me. I give you all of it, master."

Treves was not listening. He had walked a distance away from the Korean when he replied in good humor:

"Good, Chen. That's good, Chen Sin Sen! Very good!"

Through the seventeenth floor resounded the persistent ringing of a telephone. Treves entered his office and shut the door behind him. Seating himself in the padded chair, he coughed, as though about to address his employees. The ringing seemed to grow louder, rattling the window panes. With outward calm, Treves raised the receiver to his ear:

"Hello?"

The telephone operator sang out:

"You are connected with Paris. Bijour and Company calling."

A distant, pregnant silence. The silence lasted for a moment or two. In the next three minutes two people who had never seen each other and were uncertain in what language to converse, suddenly felt very near, despite the three thousand miles of ocean separating them.

"Hello? Monsieur Treves?" The voice from
Paris was a familiar one; it could have been a New
York friend speaking. "Two months ago, I would
have considered your proposition mad. Now I think
it perfectly sane—in fact, the only course of action
possible. Send the order right off. If we have to, I'll
sell the goods below the market price. Let that
modern Haman know that we Jews are not at any-
body's mercy!"

The three minutes ended. Treves kept the receiver to his ear, listening for an echo—like a man
standing in the railroad station after the departure
of someone dear to him. Joy rose in him, the joy of
creation. When the three thousand mile distance between them that had been broken for three minutes
was resumed, and buzzing assailed his ear, Treves
hung up the receiver, and leaned back in his chair.

What matter that he had just lost ten thousand
dollars? He was happy because the Jew in France
had spoken with such contempt of the modern
Haman; he was happy because Bijour too was ready
to lose money in order to defeat the enemy of the
Jews.

When Treves rose, night had fallen. Taking a
small red flag out of a box, he approached the map
of Europe. In the darkness he located Paris and
stuck the flag in it.